CHALLENGER

Other books by the Author

24 Year Colour Service

CHALLENGER

*Nick
Best Wishes
[signature] 18 May 2015.*

Gary Kent

authorHOUSE®

AuthorHouse™
1663 Liberty Drive
Bloomington, IN 47403
www.authorhouse.com
Phone: 1-800-839-8640

© 2012 by Gary Kent. All rights reserved.

No part of this book may be reproduced, stored in a retrieval system, or transmitted by any means without the written permission of the author.

Published by AuthorHouse   05/16/2012

ISBN: 978-1-4685-0370-8 (sc)
ISBN: 978-1-4685-0372-2 (hc)
ISBN: 978-1-4685-0371-5 (e)

Any people depicted in stock imagery provided by Thinkstock are models, and such images are being used for illustrative purposes only.
Certain stock imagery © Thinkstock.

Because of the dynamic nature of the Internet, any web addresses or links contained in this book may have changed since publication and may no longer be valid. The views expressed in this work are solely those of the author and do not necessarily reflect the views of the publisher, and the publisher hereby disclaims any responsibility for them.

AUTHOR'S NOTE

My story, like the title, is double-edged. It is based on fact and fiction. The facts relating to the actions are real from my own personal experiences during my time serving on the British Army Challenger Tank, in Germany. The names of the characters in my book are not real, but they do represent my own crew who I had the honour and pleasure of serving with. The fiction side of my story is compelling to the point of reality, and that it could happen.

GSK

DEDICATED TO

Wendy for enduring long hours being alone
in the writing of this book

CONTENTS

Chapter One	The Start
Chapter Two	The Road Move
Chapter Three	Defence Line
Chapter Four	First Contact
Chapter Five	Fuel Crises
Chapter Six	Half Tracked
Chapter Seven	A New Idler
Chapter Eight	Warrior
Chapter Nine	Ulta
Chapter Ten	The Doctor
Chapter Eleven	Lost
Chapter Twelve	Alone
Chapter Thirteen	The Reunion
Chapter Fourteen	Death of the Warrior
Chapter Fifteen	The Pound
Chapter Sixteen	The Fog Bank
Chapter Seventeen	Empty Village
Chapter Eighteen	Elbe River
Chapter Nineteen	Last Round Fired
Chapter Twenty	Guard Room

Chapter One

The Start

Day one 25th August

Sergeant Normal seemed to wait forever, until he decided Kean must have missed again or the shell had failed to explode. Then he saw a brief shower of sparks scatter from the foredeck of the T-72's hull to the left of the driver's hatch, and almost at the same time it exploded outwards like a movie scene in slow motion. He saw the two hatches on the turret fly upwards, followed by the turret itself and the drivers and engine hatches. Soundlessly, to Normal, the hull tore apart, belching a swirling orb of flame. He heard Kean's awed voice:" "My God". As all ways Trooper Monty Kean never let his commander Sgt Normal down with his shooting, he was a fine Gunner, one of the best in the Squadron. Good Battle Run "if I say it myself", thought Sgt Normal. The troop had been waiting for most of the day to complete this battle run and it paid off as the troop showed the rest of the SQN that they were the best when it came to the ranges. The Brigadier was most impressed with my C/S (call sign) as he said and I quote "it was one of the best battle runs he had seen"; "well good for him I thought—that shall now cost me a round of drinks in the mess, cheers, and it won't be him paying for it."

Sergeant Rota Normal serving with one of the 3rd Armoured Tank Regiment in Germany has been in BAOR for almost 3 years of a 6 year posting. Life in Germany is what you make it and he currently lived life to the full when of duty, but when it comes to playing with these tanks his gives a 100% competent. Theirs nothing better than seating in the Commanders seat of a 60 tonne Challenger Mk 1 Tank. Its one of the finest fighting machines to come into service with the army. Sgt Normal had served on the old Chieftain so he had seen the best of both of them. God bless technology.

As well as Sgt Normal being pressed for a good shoot, his Gunner Trooper Kean got a pat on the back along with his Op LCPL

Dave Tuesday for quick loading drill. Trooper Harry Young the crews Challengers driver, treated his C/S better than he teats his own car. Still he is a fine driver. With the de-brief and the pats on the back finished with Sgt Normal took the troop back to the holding area. The troop had another road move to repair for and another Battle Run here at Bergen-Hohne. Sgt Normal told Trooper Young to make sure we were fit; any faults report them to CPL (Corporal) Staple Jones. LT Small (Lieutenant) Sgt Normal troop leader called me over "Sgt Normal can you lead the troop for the next road move" "Yes Sir" "What up sir", "flap on, I have to go for a 'o' group—should catch you up at the next range" "okay sir."

Sgt Normal's troop had heard rumours that some thing was wrong though the BFBS. They had been saying all day that a large build up of military movement has been deploying on the boarders of Germany. It had started weeks before the troop had got to Hohne concerning oil in the Middle East. The British Government were saying that the oil crisis was getting critical with parts of the oil wells drying up. The Balkans states in the East where the worst hit. There's was a state of up rising with in it own boarders and was spilling over to neighbouring countries. Thing's were coming to a head and it be us to sort it. Normal thought that he "wouldn't be surprised if our range day was called off—he just had that feeling."

The troop road move was planed for 19.30hrs. Normal had plenty of time to make sure his troop call sign's where ready. Before the road move Normal gathered the troop for a briefing, telling them that the Troop Leader had to go for a 'o' group. Trooper Kean wonted to know what was going down, as well as the rest of the Troop. "Honest lads I am in the dark as you are—if I can find any thing out you'll be the first to know." "Now stop moaning and get these vehicles ready", "all I won't is a bloody beer" Monty said, don't we all.

Once the troop had reached the next range they were guided into the firing bays by the SQN SSM ready for the following day shoot. CPL Jones went round the troop to carry out a full halt parade on the entire troop challengers; it had been a long road move the first such move for a long time. It did the Challenges good to burn a bit of rubber He came back with a small list. The major fault was Sgt Norma's call sign, it had a suspension leak on the third road station, not a major fault but it needed to be sorted out. Gone were the days of the old fashion spring pack's which helped the vehicle run smoother over rough terrain. These Challengers had this new Hydro Gas suspension unit. It was a good system when it worked it made the vehicle rise once the gas warmed up, plus it was a lot smoother ride when driving cross country.

After Rota had looked at the list from Staple he went over to the LAD and saw SSGT Eagles. "Hi Rota" he said. "Now Les, been busy mate"! SSGT Eagles was seating in the back of his 432 having a beer, "alright for some" said Rota. Les turned round and offered one to Rota "no thanks mate better keep a clear head—you never know what's round the corner". Rota handed the list over; Les said "he would send some one over". Once Rota had said good bye to Les he wondered over to find the SQN Sargent Major. Vance Key was having a fag and cuppa when he got to him. Vance looked up when he was near him; Vance handed over a fag and told his driver to make him a cuppa. Rota handed him the same fault list for the troop, so he could collate all the troops vehicle sates for the SQN LDR "thanks Rota". "You had a good shoot today mate" said Vance. "All part of the training" said Rota—He wonted to ask what the flap was all about but thought better of it. Before he left Vance took him by the arm and said "take care Rota remember your drills mate if you need help you know where I am"—"strange I thought why say that, he knows some thing". Vance eyes said it all—but what?

Back with the troop CPL Jones told Rota that a runner had come from SHQ to say "that the SQN LDR wonted all SQN call sign's to be 100% by 0800 hrs. Tomorrow morning". Cpl Jones came over and said "that his—plus the Troop Leader call sign were ready." "Okay Staple" "you take the rest of the troop for a beer; I shall catch you up once we get this suspension fixed". As soon as they had got on the transport the LAD came," typical said Mounty "now we have to wait for the next transport to arrive" It didn't take them long to pump more gas into the system once they replaced a valve.

On arrival back to barracks it was straight down to the cellar bar for a well deserved drink, of cold Beer. All the SQN was in the bar as the SSM had passed the word that the SQN LDR was coming down to give the SQN a brief. "Better get some more beer in then" said Mounty—"Serge you won't another"— "yer go on then—thanks."

SQN LDR Bucket came though the door with the 2i/c, they didn't look to happy. "Stand up Gentlemen", said the SSM, "carry on Sargent Major". The bar was quite you could have heard a pin drop. First the SQN LDR congratulated the SQN on an excellent days shooting, Out lining that the top Troop was 3 Troop, cheers went up, more rounds were needed, but that had to wait. Now for the gritty business of why we were having this brief. As we have all heard listening to what has been said though the BFBS, the crises over the oil has worsted. To that end the remaining range days have been cancelled, all Sqn MBT will be Bomb, up tomorrow morning, with live rounds. That started the chit chat, "quite said the SSM". Once this has been completed the SQMS shall replen all Challengers. Each troop shall be issued spare parts, such as fan belts, filters and oil. Once this has been done, at 1300hrs the RTC (Royal Corp of Transport) shall be arriving to transport the SQN to Berg. There we shall take up a defensive position and wait further orders from brigade. Gentlemen that is all the news I have if I find out more I shall pass it down to you though your Troop Leader, s—any question? Trooper Young raised his hand "Sir" "what about our wife's back home". The Regiment, so the SQN LDR said "has laid on extra transport to take them all to Bligh tie" "Gentlemen this situation my, worsen to the extent that we not see our love ones for some time". SQN LDR Bucket final words were that he was proud of being your SQN LDR and as far as he was concerned he had the best SQN in the regiment and he new what ever we shall encounter, we shall do our best.

Once the SQN LDR had gone Rota got up from the table, he looked at his troop of young faces all where deep in thought and then made his way to the Sqn bar, this is going to be one hell of a night; we might not get another one for some time he thought. Most of the lads legged it to find a phone. Sgt Normal was once married and they had two kids, she the wife took them back to England, when they split up over two years ago. Now what the Sqn Ldr had said he thought that he should have made more of an effort and have spent more time with them, now it seemed that Normal might not see them again—He should write them all a long letter once he got back to his room, he told him self. The Troop got hammered then staggered back to the block to sleep it of, not knowing what tomorrow shall bring.

Chapter Two

The Road Move

Day Two 26th August

    3Troop staged out of the accommodation block ready for the transport to arrive to take them to the range, more score heads than normal were had ready for first parade, which was at the firing point. Not much was said on the transport. The Troop didn't have long to wait until the SQMS arrived with his merry men, along with the Ammo. They had to de—bomb the challenger's first as they all had the normal range ammo on board. It didn't take the Troop long even thou they all had hag overs to get the 64 rounds stowed away. The break down the Troop had was 40 rounds of APFSDS and 24 of HESH along with boxes of 7.62 for both coax machine guns, 5.65mm for the personnel weapons not for getting the bag charges and vent tube rounds, and most of all the lads stowed away a few bottle's of beer from the night before. After that came the POL (Petrol Oil Lubricant) "we were certainly being looked after" said Mounty Kean, god knows when we shall see the SQMS again.
    SQN LDR Bucket made his way down the line; of Challenger's he looked like he had been up all night. A lot of reasonability hug on his shoulders, thought Rota. When he came to the troop he had a smile on his face-good morning Sgt Normal every thing alright, "yes Sir all the ammo and rations are on board". "Do you think well shall be using them sir"?, "what the ration Sgt Normal, no I know what you mean and yes am afraid to say—you shall." "Can you tell us any more news sir"? "No sorry Brigade is keeping quite at the moment". "What I have heard is that the Governments are trying to resolve the crises, that much is clear as I know it". As Sgt Normal saluted the SQN LDR he returned the complement then made his way to the next troop, he was one of the best officers which Rota had, had the pleasure of working with.

Not long after the SQN LDR had gone, the Troop got another runner from SHQ. He brought them up to date maps of the area they were going to, along with frequencies for the radios and passwords. He said they shall last 72hours until we received more from the regiment HQ. "They must think its going to be a quick war", "that's if it turns into a war" said Harry Young. Along with the maps, they gave us all a grid which would act as a ground dump location which we plotted on the new maps. "It was quite a distance from our defensive position", said Cpl Jones. Rota turned round and said "that all areas had been carefully worked out, the SQMS and his merry men had one hell of a road move to the dump still he would be better of than us, by the sounds of things" Cpl Staple Jones gave Rota a long hard stare, he thought was all this for real. With a full tank of diesel on board which was about 1300ltr it give the troop a road distance of roughly 450km, if they decided to go cross country then the Troop was looking at a distance of 250km ish.

The RCT turned up with their transporters this was beginning to make things all that real. Trooper Harry Young followed his transport ready to be guided on. Once he managed to land with out falling of, the Call sign's was shackled down ready for the long rod move. All crews were told that they would all be mounted with there own C/S. The last time Rota did this was back in the 70s with exercise Lion Hart. Sgt Normal made his way and found Lt Small and CPL Jones; he wonted to make sure they were ready to go. Sgt Normal mentioned that they could use there GUE on the way as it would be quite a while before we had a pit stop.

Rota said his good byes and then walked down the line of Challenger Tanks until he found his own C/S as Rota climbed aboard he felt the cold damp of security of the Challengers armour against his body, it felt safe but on the other hand it felt like he was entombed. As Rota sat back in his commander's seat there were sounds, unnatural and muffled yet familiar to him; the stifled movement of men, whispered conversations, a throat softly cleared, equipment adjusted and the unliveable sense that some one talking to him, "fancy a drink sarge" said Dave Tuesday—"thanks mate".

Trooper Harry Young piped up and said "how long shall we be in this tin can"? "As long as it takes and a bit more, bloody fantastic, I better get my head down then". Not long after you heard the trickle of urine being emptied into a tin can—how apt. Rota placed his feet on the breach block ready for the long hall and closed his eyes.

Intelligence indicated that a major enemy thrust was likely to be made at the point where the areas of responsibility of the NATO forces overlapped were upon the plan was to channel the main thrust to the densely forested areas to the north of Celle. It was wisely known that this was a tank training ground for the German army since the days of Third Reich, so what was then good for them surely it must be good for us—we hope.

After what seemed ages cramped in side this tin can Trooper Harry Young piped up and said "sarge when are we going to have a pit stop". He must have just woken up as he sounded grumpy, not a good start to what lay ahead of us. "When you feel the vehicle stop then you know it's the time okay"—"okay sarge".

As it was they did stop. Rota opened his hatch it was good to feel fresh air on his face. It had started to drizzle lightly, rain as fine as mist, and now there was the sharp chill of autumn approaching and the metallic scent of damp woodland in the air. As Sgt Normal climbed out, the cupola hatch he noticed that all crews from the Sqn had started to emerge from the glom of the turret; it was like a seen from the living dead. Rota got a nock on his leg, it was Trooper Mounty Kean, Rota stood on top of Challenger to let him out, and Rota noticed that they had parked near wood land, hence the damp woodland in the air. They were told that the stop would last no longer than 30 minute. Normal walked over to see the rest of the Troop; he wonted to see how they had coped. Lt Small said his BV was U/S "had they checked the circuit breaker? Lt Small Operator came round from the back and said, "No he hadn't—okay you better check it then". He soon popped his head out the turret and said it was working now. Rota smiled and made his way to see CPL Jones. He on the other hand told him that they had no eternal water coming though so had gone with out a drink since they had been on the road. Rota pointed out that they should look at the plunger on the hose to make sure that was working—it was. Cpl Jones asked his operator did he fill up the water tank before they left the range. Along wait was observed before he finally answered along with a bright red face, he had for got, "don't worry we, all make mistakes", Rota told him, he turned then slowly walked back to his challenger, with a smile on his face.

Sgt Normal was on his way back to his own call sign when a runner came up and said that all call signs had to be unloaded ASAP. Rota didn't waste time in running back to find Lt Small and told him that the dead line for us to get to our location had been brought forward; they had to make there own way. From the SQN LDR all troops would move out in 20 minute intervals, order of match would be SHQ, 1st Troop, 2nd Troop, and then us followed by 4thTroop. With the quick brief given by Lt Small along with new secure radio frequency and passwords, he out lined the route the Troop would be taken. Sgt Normal asked the question concerning loading the main armaments; Lt Small said he would find out. He wasn't long with the answer—it was yes APFSDS to be loaded, with the vent tube loader loaded but not rammed home. This would make the main armament safe until contact was given. It brought home the reality of what was going on with us all, can this be happing here in Germany 60 Years since the last war.

Rota told the troop that they had plenty of time to have some thing to eat so get the BV on and make sure the water tanks are full up; we might not get the chance again, it was going to be a long night. Lt Small informed the Troop that in the event of any Challenger breaking down, it was the reasonability of that Call sign to try to fix it them self's before they called up for the REME. Sgt Normal wasn't too happy with this order he wasn't prepared to leave any of his Troop or challengers behind if he could help it at any cost.

Chapter Three

Defence Line

Day Three 27ᵗʰ August

H Hour was 15 minute away. Sgt Normal made his way down the long straight road to check up on each of the Troop Challengers. What Rota was going to say he had no idea? He could give them the famous message which Lord Nelson said before the battle of Trafalgar to his men, but thought better of it. In the end Sgt Normal said to them all to make sure they carried out the drills which they had been taut and all should work out fine, what a load of bull shit. No one knows what each person shall be like under fire, when it comes then you hope your training shall come to it own. Time shall tell if this statement comes true.

Trooper Harry Young said "had he got time for a dump before we sent of"? Rota said "yes" but make it a quick, he didn't take a shovel with him he just went be hide the vehicle. Great I hope he missed the track. Once Harry climbed back in Rota told him to start up, the sound was like being in a formula one car nothing could match this sound. After Trooper Mounty Kean had started his gun kit Rota told Trooper Dave Tuesday to load APFSDS but not to ram the vent tube loader, Rota also told him to make ready the CO-AX GPMG.

Lt Small was leading so Normal just settled back in his seat and started to drift of into his own world. Rota looked up and amide the clear sky it was turning from a bright clear sky to a dark cold unwelcome sight it sent shivers down his back, snap out of it he told him self but the thought of what might come kept him in his wonder world for a few more minutes until Trooper Young brought the reality back. He told Rota that the Troop Leader had stopped. Rota noticed that the Troop Leader had pulled over to the side of the road he told Harry Young to pull up behind him. Once they had come to a halt Rota quickly grab, his webbing and ran towards the Troop Leader. He was half way down when Rota reached him. "What's up sir"? Lt

Small said that his driver had said that his main oil pressure warring light had come on. "Okay sir, tells your gunner to traverse rear so I can get the decks up". It wasn't long before Rota found the fault the right hand fan belt had sheared off. Good job we carried spares so the task could be done with out the REME thought Rota. With the help of the driver they soon got it replaced, it was bloody hot work all the same. While this was going on the last Troop in the SQN had passed them, by the time they had finished it was 3 Troop which was the rear Troop. Once they were motoring again the Troop made up for the lost time with out any further incidents. It wasn't long before Rota realised that they had came to the hide location for the night. Lt Small was met by the SSM who informed the Troop leader that due to high volume of traffic, and the fact that they were the rear Troop he was to take his Troop to the secondary hide which was about another 30km away; there they should be met by the RMP to guide them in to your location. Dave Tuesday was standing half out of his hatch, watching the night sky towards the west. Flashes of distant light flickered like summer lightning along the horizon, and the sky itself was coloured as though it reflected the illumination of a vast city. It was almost beautiful to watch the clouds glowing scarlet in the far distance place. Rota soon came upon the RMPs. They told the Tpr Ldr. where to go and informed him that they had company to our right flak part of the 7th German Armoured which was nice to hear. Sgt Normal stared down across the long easy slope towards the frontier. The ridge commanded a board open section of the plain between two small hamlets. A stream only visible through binoculars and little more than six meters in width defied the distant border, meandering its way between East and West. Northwards was rich flat farmland, interposed with bands of young pine forests. "It's a good position the RMP informed Sgt Normal. Not long after Rota noticed that the RMP had soon legged it once they had finished with the Troop Leader. The Troop found good hull down positions and was prepared for any thing and a long night. No need for ground sentries as the infantry were dug in all around us, Rota noticed a few of their Warriors. Dave Tuesday was still looking at the bright coloured sky, until Rota told him to get the BV on, "it is on", he said "well make us a brew Dave" said Harry Young. The brew was soon made and passed down to Trooper Young. It wasn't long before they heard this gurgling sound coming from

Harry's drivers' compartment. Mounty Kean shouted down and said "what the hell are you doing Harry, cleaning your bloody teeth"? "Yes why"? You be bloody shaving next then—"I have done" in what then your tea. Rota thought god what a crew he had, Rota only wished Trooper Kean would change his pants.

It seemed like eternity since they arrived here but the reality was only a few hours. Sgt Normal soon had had a visit from the infantry commander, asking if could observer this gird which they had been observing for some while during day light hours. Rota told Mounty to lie on and see what he could see. His TOGS (Thermal Observation Gunnery System) didn't revel any thing which was out the ordinary; the infantry commander thanked us, but asked us to keep an eye on it. Both radios nets had been quite for a while, so Rota decided to make his way over to see the Tpr Ldr. He too was concerned that they had not heard any news. Lt Small told Sgt Normal that due to his break down we were now the forward Troop of the SQN which meant we where out here on our own. Rota asked LT Small if the infantry had been over for a chat. He said they had and were due to pull out in the next hour, which meant we had to post a stag rota then? LT Small said we should just stay crew mounted until first light, and then decide. "Okay sir I shall tell CPL Jones on what is going on then"? "Okay Sgt Normal and say we shall use the troop chatter net to keep in contact with each other during the night". Sgt Normal soon found CPL Jones challenger which was some distances from the other two. He was busy eating when Rota got there, his driver saw him coming as he was having a shovel recce. Rota climbed aboard and told Staple what he new which wasn't a lot. Staple seemed to be doing okay. CPL Jones asked "if we should ram home the vent tube, you never know" he said "it might save pressure us seconds". Rota told him to get on to the Tpr Ldr and see what he had to say. The Tpr Ldr soon came back and said ram them home. That was it then, only thing left was to make the loaders guard and bam wham war has started, for 3 Troop

Rota walked back towards his challenger as he climbed back board he could hear talking coming though the loaders hatch which wasn't very technical, what the lads were talking about, he hand no idea. They soon shut up as his boots hit his seat. Rota was handed a brew, along with a fag, it came with smiles on there faces, what going on then they asked. Mounty said "that Harry Young had changed his coveralls but hasn't got any more under Pat's left". It was a question which had to asked, so I asked Trooper Young "why he had no pants left", he had used his last par to wipe his bum as he couldn't find the loo roll in time. Great still it was good to see that the lads were in good humour. Rota gave the order to Trooper Tuesday to ram home the vent tube loader; he looked at me and just shrugged his shoulders giving me the impression that he didn't give a dam. What's wrong Dave? He was thinking of his wife and kids and wondering if he shall see them again. Rota told Dave and the rest of the crew that what ever happens he shall make sure you all shall see your love ones again—that I promise. Silence hit the tank after that last remark all in our own dreams of the loved ones that they had left be hind. It was broken by the Tpr Ldr coming on the net telling Rota that they shall be pulling out at first light. The next location was going to be the Elbe River. We had a few hours left before first light it would be stupid in not taking these hours to catch up on sleep, so let's make the most of it, said Rota. The crew was split up into pars, with Harry Young and Normal to gather witched left Dave Tuesday and Monty Kean

Silence fill again in the glom of the turret, it was broken by the snoring sound coming from the depths with in.

Chapter Four

First Contact

Day four 27th August

The weather was fine with a slight mist hanging around once we came out of our firing positions. It had been a long night with out any incident. Normal opened his hatch looking around he found that the troop where the only friendly call signs left, had they all been asleep and not realised what had taken part. Sgt Normal checked on Lt Small It wasn't long before he came back to say that they should pull out. The Troop soon came across its first village which was surrounded by rolling hill; it looked a picture of beauty, but it was deserted apart from the odd dog roaming the now empty streets looking for it master. It was an aerie sight to witness where the villages had gone was any body's guess. They didn't stop for any saviours going though the village we pushed on as fast as they could.

Trooper Young piped up and said "could we stop for a pee", Rota said "cart you do it a bottle then"? "I have and now have run out of things to pee in". Okay, Rota told Mounty to traverses off a bit so that Dave Tuesday could past down this bean can which they had for breakfast, "thanks Sarge". Dave piped up and commentated that Harry wouldn't have a problem getting his pecker out now that he isn't wearing any pants; they just bust out laughing at the thought of it. It's a good job we still had our sense of humour.

Lt Small came on the troop net and said "we should turn of now as we had passed the village". "The SQN should be hold up about 25kms in the secondary location, so going over the rolling hills it should cut the time down by half, plus it would be quicker if headed direct, in stead of following the road". He made sense some time and this was one of those occasions. Once the troop had hit the cross country they formed up as a diamond formation. Sgt Normal had a quick look at his map and noticed that the SQN should be over the next rise. Rota got on the troop net and told the Tpr Ldr that they should creep up to the next rise and have a look see. Looking though his sights Rota didn't notice a signal SQN vehicle. Rota asked LT Small if he had seen what I had—he had nothing. Sgt Normal said that he would go down and see what had happed to the SQN, you and CPL Jones can act FSC (Fire Support Control). Rota told his crew what was going on, they new as they could here the chat on the net, still it didn't matter keeping them up to speed. Rota told Harry to revise then swing hard right stick which bought them around the rise and in to dead ground. They soon made it to the SQN hide which was empty. Normal entered the wood and found a good support position to guide the rest of the troop in. Once the rest had turned up and found a suitable position, Rota dismounted and made my way to LT Small. Lt Small was grabbing his webbing once Rota reached him. Well sir "looks like they have done a runner", "it seems so Sgt Normal" we better have a look around you never know they might have left us some thing. On the first search they reviled nothing. It wasn't until one of CPL Jones crew went for a shovel recce did he find the empty 7.62am mo box. He bought it back pleased as punch he had found it. In side it was a batco message it was like being in the MI5 all this clock and dagger crap. Trooper Tuesday decoded it; it informed them of a new gird to head for. Again it was heading back closer to the Elbe. Rota asked Trooper Tuesday if any thing was on either of the radios—there wasn't. It didn't make sense they hadn't had a radio message since they started this crusade. Sgt Normal made his way over to see LT Small's operator. He found him in side the turret making a brew. "Hi Sarge fancy one", "no thanks mate". "When you got the radio frequencies from SHQ did they say how long they would last for"? "24 hours and we should receive new ones at our first hide". Did the SSM give you any when he spoke with the Tpr Ldr, "no Sarge", okay "thanks?" Sgt Normal climbed back down and found LT Small with CPL Jones. "Sir we have a bloody problem". "What that's then"? Sgt Normal went on to explain about the radio frequencies. The look on LT Small face said it all. The troop was on its own with no help or support from any one. "What the fuck are we going to do now Sgt Normal"? The only option we have is to make our way back to this last grid reference in this ammo box and hope we come across our own lines. If we hadn't gone further on to that hide we would have received our new frequencies, what a fuck up.

Trooper Young came running over and said the word that would change there situation for some time to come-CONTACT.

With the Troop Leader and CPL Jones Rota edge closer to the edge of the wood. Coming towards them was a T80 with two BTR 70, they seemed to be following our tracks. Mount up lads, said Rota. Once Rota had climbed back on his own Challenger the face of Trooper Young had changed, he gave him the thumbs up sign he in turn returned the jester. Sgt Normal got on the troop net and told the rest of the troop that he would take out the T80 the other two consecrate on the BTR 70s. The BRT 70s had a 14.5mm gun fitted to its turret and could give them a nasty head ach. Rota told Mounty to lie on the T80 turret ring, Dave Tuesday shouted loaded, they were ready. Lt Small and CPL Jones came over the net and said there were all so ready. FIRE shouted Sgt Normal—LASING—FIRING NOW shouted Mounty. The wait seemed to take for ages until Mounty shouted TARGET. Looking through the sights at the burning hulk it didn't seem real what they had done. The turret had flown a good 20 metres away from the rest of the body. The other two targets were also burning; CPL Jones had opened up with his CO-AX to finish of the crew's which had managed to escape from the rear. The engagement had lasted no more than five minutes. Reality made Sgt Normal come back to earth with a bump. He told Harry to revise and to follow the edge of the wood until we came to the clearing, LT Small and Cpl Jones was soon following. They were burning track rubber like they had no tomorrow. Rota new that they had to make a good distance from the last engagement, he also new that the enemy would have got of there own contact report, once they had opened up on them.

Dark clouds hug over the seen as they left, as if some one new that people had died. The light was soon turning into a dark lest aerie night with out the moon to show the way. The map indicated that there was a large wooded area about 20 clicks away from us. Sgt Normal got on the Troop net and quickly briefed LT Small to follow him to the next location. The 20 clicks were done in quick time no hanging about; the Challengers were flying and had soon reached the night location. Normal decided that the troop should park near the front of the wood but at the same time keeping under cover in case they should have to make a run for it. Cpl Jones once he had parked up organised the sentry post, he put his own crew on first stag. Troopers Young went round and told the other drivers to do a quick halt parade.

Sgt Normal webbing was hanging on the rear antenna which made it easy for him to grab. Rota and made his way to the sentry post he wonted to make sure that they were okay.

When he reached them they were beside them self's talking about the engagement. Normal told them to keep the noise down a bit, he then turned away and smiled to him self knowing that they where okay.

The Troop Leader came running over when he spotted Sgt Normal coming back. "Sgt Normal" said the Tpr Ldr "what a hell of an engagement we have just had", it seemed to Rota that the Troop Leader was on a high. "Yes Sir the Troop did us proud". Rota handed him a fag, thanks. After he had had a few puffs Rota noticed his hands had stopped shacking. Normal looked over his shoulder to see what the troop were doing, they were doing what he had trained them to do, and that was to get on with it. Dave Tuesday came over with a brew and a sandwich. Rota nodded his thanks and then watched him return to his Challenger. Rota couldn't have asked for a better crew than the one he had now.

Sgt Rota Normal waved Cpl Staple Jones over, once he arrived he told him along with the Troop Leader that they should hold up here for the night to let the situation calm down a bit before they moved out again. Rota said that we three should do the radio watch while the rest of the lads got there heads down, what lay before us tomorrow morning was any bodies guess. Lt Small said they should head for the last know grid which the Squadron was aiming for before this shit came down on us. Rota said he would work out a route plain, once he had made it he would come round and find them. Before they left Rota said while they were on stag they should switch on the TOGS (Thermal Observation Gunnery System) as all three Challengers had turrets front, they could traverse by hand if they had to.

Rota was woken up by Cpl Jones. He pulled down his zip of his sleeping bag; the air was full of moister and he felt that his maggot was damp with it. He climbed on top of the NBC pack and entered the dark cold turret; he found the master switch to illuminate the turret and quickel turned down the dimmer control. Rota climbed over the breech to get to his commanders seat and switched on his TOGS. Looking though his sights he noticed a world of wild life how strange it seemed that just a few hours ago he was looking at the enemy though the same sight now he was watch a fox cleaning it self. Rota looked at his watch and noticed it was 3 am only 1 1/2 hours to go plenty of time to get my head down again before we moved of again. Looking though his sights he saw flashes far away in the distance some poor sod is getting pounded he thought.

Dawn came too soon it was time to do catch up, but not before we had a cuppa. Lt Small came over while Rota was having his brew. "Morning Sgt Normal" "morning Sir" remarked Rota. The Tpr Ldr decided that they should travel by day and rest up by night. It wasn't like being on exercise you tend to know where the enemy was; now we were looking for a needle in a hay stack. By using the dead ground and surround areas we should be able to keep out of trouble. Most of our training involved leap fogging from bound to bound, this meant we would have one foot on the ground at all times. It was slow moving but a better way of keep safe.

The troop was ready Rota said he would lead. Rota first bound wasn't long so we kept this up for most of the day with out having any contact. Sgt Normal last bound was over looking a small village surround by wood land. He told Trooper Young to give him a turret up position, once Kean was happy he told Harry to stop. We both had a good look though our sights and the seen was that of devastation. Most if not all the houses had been set alight. Mounty Kean noticed that the streets were lettered with the dead. Normal got on to the troop net and told the other two what to expect, it wasn't going to be very pleasant. Mounty had kept his eyes glued to his sights and had noticed movement in one of the gardens near to them. Kean nudged the legs of his commander. "What's up Mounty", "take a look is all he said". Rota pushed his eyes to his sight as far as they would go what he saw was a group of solders running after some thing, the thing turned out to be a young woman in her 20s who was completely naked. They soon caught her up then the torment started. They circled her like a pack of wide wolfs so she couldn't move and started to pass her around the circle. On the out side of this torment stood a lonely figure that seemed to be the head poncho. He gave some quick orders to four of his men who then grab the women and pushed her to the floor. Rota noticed that each man held a limb of the woman; the ones who held the legs forced her to open them. You could image the seen from with in the turret, Lt Small and Cpl Jones reported that no further movement was noticed in the village, this gave the signal that Rota had been waiting for. He told Mounty to laser the basted then finish them of with CO-AX. Mounty didn't fuck about he had finished them of with in 5 minutes. Rota gazed though his commanders' sight at the carnage which was left, nothing was standing. Mounty shouted that the young woman was moving. It turned out that she hadn't been hit and had managed to free her self from the fallen. She looked round before legging it towards the wood in the far distance. What became of her they never found out?

    Sgt Normal got on the net and suggested that they should do a recce to find out who those fuckers where. Rota took Dave Tuesday with him. Mounty climbed up into the commanders' seat. Rota and Dave grab they webbing and small arms and made there way to the seen. All the dead had the same flasher showed on there uniform's they belong to a Mechanize Artillery Brigade. They may have been the same ones who had encaged us before. They made their way towards the centre of the village, what they saw made them sick. All the villages had been shot, the women where all naked even the very young girls. Okay Dave we have seen what we have come to see lets get back, but before Rota got the last word out they came under attack from small arms fire coming from the direction of the church tower. They returned fire and started to move back towards the Challengers. Inside the turret Mounty had seen the engagement and had let rip the main armament using HESH. Not much was left of the church tower or the sniper. Rota and Dave picked them self's up and legged it back, not before a BMP popped its head around a corner and op-ed up with a .50 calibre gun. They needn't have worried as Mounty had seen the BMP at the same time and had put a round right up its tail pipe.

Sgt Normal gave the Troop Leader a quick brief on the situation once he climbed back inside the confinements of his Challenger. Lt Small mentioned that it was time to find a good location again for a night hide before it gets to dark. They both studied the map and noticed a large wooded area a good distance away. Lt Small lead the way while Rota shorted him self out then he to revised and followed on, leaving the dead far be hind him.

Chapter Five

Fuel Crises

Day five 28th August

Sgt Rota Normal left the village far behind him with thoughts of what had just taken place, and wounded if the next village would be the same. While they had been in the hide the night before Sgt Normal guested that most of the advancing troops had over taken them and they were now truly behind enemy lines, just like the movies but this was reality.

It wasn't long before Rota realised that they had reached the troop location for the night as the Troop Leader came on the net stating that the hide looked okay. Cpl Jones reversed his Challenger in first followed by Lt Small. Sgt Normal told Harry Young to run up and down the side of the wood to disguised the track marks of the other two, once he was happy he told Harry Young to revers his own Challenger into the dark glum of the wood. Rota looked around the depth of the wood and was happy with all the position, then he gave the signal for the troop to switch off the engines. Silence fell upon them again like it had done the night before and would continue to do so for nights to come. For a few solitary moments in time Sgt Normal just sat in his commander's seat and differed of in to his own world away from the carnage of what he had just witnessed. It did not last for long; Mounty Kean taped his leg indicating that he wonted to get out. Sgt Normal stood on his turret watching his crew carrying on with the tasks that all ways befell a troop once it occupied a hide. Troop Young looked up at Rota and said "do we need to do the cam net"? Sgt Normal smiled and replied "no mate not to night".

The troop hide was soon set up. Cpl Staple Jones had posted the ground sentries and had used the Don10 to cornet to the operator who was on radio watch all seemed to be okay thought

Rota. Lt Small came over and asked if the crew was okay, referring to what had been. Sgt Normal looked at him and replied that his crew was fine. Before Rota could continue talking with his Troop Leader Cpl Jones came running up with the troop fault list and handed them to Sgt Normal. All three Challengers needed to be refuelled and Lt Small challenger needed to have a link taken out on each track. This would not cause a problem if they were back in camp, but here with in the glum of the wood they would have a problem. The troop needed to find a suitable location of frim ground, here in the hide the ground looked sodded they had the space but it was the noise that worried Sgt Normal. Carrying out this task out during the night wasn't an option. LT Small said they should wait until the morning, for once he said the right words. The troop looked knackered what they wonted was sleep so if they where not on stag then it was get your head down.

Sgt Normal took LT Small by the arm and walked away from the rest of the troop. Trooper Kean nodded at Harry Young in a way that asked the question what they are up to then. Harry Young shrugged his shoulders in response, he new that his vehicle commander would tell him when he got back.

Rota offered the troop leader a fag which he took, clasping his hands over the lighter to shield the light he drew a deep breath in to inhale the smoke then blew it out which dwarfed into the night sky. "What's up Rota asked the Troop Leader", "Sir it the state of the fuel which we have left". "If we cart find some soon then we shall be walking back to the Elbe bearing in mind we have not had a replen since we left the rangers". "What do you suggest we do"? "Two option, one is to carry on until we run dry second is to locate a sauce were we can get diesel from". "You seem to have some thing in mind Sgt Normal concerning the later" suggestion said LT Small. Rota smiled he knew the troop leader could read him like a book that's what made them a work well together. Sgt normal went on to say what he had in mind. He had noticed that out side the last village which they had came across was a large barn which looked like it housed the local framers machines, and at the side of the barn was the framers own fuel tank how apt. Lt Small said it would be un wise to travel back to that village with what had happened, Rota agreed but carried on in saying that from here until they reached the Elbe their must be dozen of farm buildings like that it was a question of finding one and quick. Once back at his Challenger Dave Tuesday was still up, Rota asked him he had any doubts which he might what to get of his chest, Dave turned round and said "that all was well he had stayed up to give his commander his supper". Rota thanked him and watched him crawl into his sleeping bag. It brought home how lucky he was to have such a crew as the one he had now; he promised them that he would get them all back home. Rota climbed into his turret as it was his turn to do a radio stag; he had a lot to think about and to sort out.

It was raining hard when Sgt Normal pulled down his zipper of his sleeping bag, great he thought not a good start to the day. Rota jumped of the rear decks to have a pee and noticed that the Challenger had suck during the night. No track bashing to day then. The rain which had fallen during the night had made the ground that soft even the boots of Mounty Kean had suck into the ground when he to jumped of the tank. Harry Young mentioned to Sgt Normal that if the Troop Leader didn't watch were he was driving he would pull a track off. The decision was made for him that they had to find a barn. During his radio watch he had noticed that a small hamlet was about 30 kms away they may have what they are looking for.

Sgt Normal told his crew to mount up. He made his way to the Troop Leader and Cpl Jones. Once there he informed them of what he had in mind, they were all in agreement. Rota ran back and gave Harry Young the signal to crank over the engines. Once the GUE had been put on Mounty Kean didn't waste any time in starting the gun kit up. He traversed left and right to let Rota know that he was ready. Harry Young told his commander that all system were working down the engine room, Rota reply was telling Young that it was a Challenger tank he was driving not a bloody battleship Mounty looked over the breach and smiled at Dave Tuesday. Sgt Normal eased his challenger out the hide first to take a hull down position allowing the other two to leap fog to the next bound. In this way the troop would all ways have a fume footing on the ground at any one time. The first bound was kept short as it all depended on the ground. They had no contact which was good. The Troop was coming to the last bound which Sgt Normal would do before finally reaching the village. Rota told Harry to cheep forward to the next rise, Mounty yelled okay Harry. The challenger stopped with a launch forward on it suspension. Silence befell the turret crew before Rota called up the other two to have a look. Rota watched the other Challengers cheep forward like a well oiled machine.

Mounty had noticed a large barn on the other side of the village, while waiting for the rest of the Troop. Monty tapped his commander's leg; Rota then had a look through his own sight, at what Monty had seen. Rota had noticed that the dead ground to the barn would act as good cover for approach. Rota called up CPL Jones on the Troop net asking him he had seen the barn at the far side of the village, CPL Jones said "he had seen it, use the dead ground to get their then give us a call on the Troop net, roger that—out". Sgt Normal twisted his neck to watch him pull away by using his cupola sights, he used the dead ground very well thought Rota. It wasn't long before Staple Jones came on the net and informed the Troop that it was clear. Lt Small answered "Roger that, moving in 3", "Roger"—Staple acknowledged. The two remaining Challengers soon made the distance towards the barn. Both Challengers drove straight in. Inside the space was found to be huge it housed the farmers machine by the equipment which had been left be hind. Normal dismounted from his Challenger grabbing his webbing on the way. He wonted to make sure that it would safe to carry out the track bashing. He told the other vehicle commanders that the gunners could do the first stag while the drivers carried on with the task in had.

Un known to the Troop they had been spotted driving in to the barn. It wasn't long before the locals paid them a visit. Trooper Kean spotted them coming over the field and gave the heads up that we had visitors. The two men and one woman just entered the barn; they did not look surprised at seeing us. One of the men was the local mayor of the village the other man was just an escort, the woman well she could speak good English.

The mayor informed us that they had been visited by the eastern block soldiers and had stayed for two days. Lt Small asked him when they had left; he said "that it wasn't long roughly between 2-3 hours". The woman took over with the story in saying "once they had come most of the men had been out attending the field, they had been the lucky ones" she said. The woman started to cry so the mayor placed his hand on her shoulder for comfort. After she had composed her self she carried on with the story. She went on to say "that they had rounded up all the villages young and old, and brought them to the village centre". "Then it started, the rape, murder, and the torcher they just turned the village into a blood bath for no reason at all". Rota asked her "if she had been raped", she said "that her and her sisters had been attending the cattle, but had witnessed it all once they came back to the village". They had managed to hide for two days before they left. Rota wonted to know why the mayor had been spared. She looked to wards the mayor with sadness in her face and said "with out looking at Rota she said that they wonted him to watch and witness what they were about to do". They tied him to a chair so he couldn't escape, he was their, until she realised him. The captain had ordered that two of the village be brought before him they picked on two of the younger men. Once they had been kicked and punched the captain walked up to them and asked "Where are your companions". Then young men did not answer. The captain then turned around and made his way towards the mayor. He wisped some thing into his ear then laughed. He then made his way back to the centre of the square to were, the young me where, he suddenly stepped forward and kicked the young man in the groin. He shrieked in pain and almost passed out but the captain slapped his face to keep him conscious. The captain kept on repeating the same question and once more received silence in answer. This seemed to madden the captain more who then snatched the guard's weapon from one of his men. With all his strength, he drove the butt into the man's groin, smashing it repeatedly into that most sensitive area until the scrotum split open. From the gaping rent, blood gushed freely, staining the village square beneath and, as the captain continued to drive the butt home one shattered testicle was torn from the man's scrotum. The purple, egg-shaped object dropped below him. Blood gushed down the young man's leg and his body twitched madly even though he was unconscious. The Captain had finished striking the young man and then handed the blood-covered weapon back to the guard. The captain turned and smiled at the mayor and said "now the second young man shall talk" The second young man didn't know the question or answer either his fate was much quicker with a bullet through his head. He had been though hell and back as he had seen his wife raped then killed. Normal looked at the rest of the Troop who had gathered round to listen to this story there faces said it all. Lt Small looked at the mayor and asked the woman to say how sorry we all were, if we can help then please lets us know. The mayor turned to towards the Troop and said revenge. Silence befell the bran before the other man said "if we can help you, then what we have is yours". Sgt Normal looked deep into the woman's eyes he could see sorrow in her face but couldn't do any thing for her. Cpl Staple asked the mayor if they had any diesel to spare. The mayor laughed out loud and said that they had plenty to give them. "What so funny" asked Lt Small he said that they too wonted fuel, when we said no then the carnage started. Why didn't you just let them have it? They didn't say please the mayor said. Normal could not believe what he had just heard; the Mayor had let all this carnage happen because of a signal word of please.

    The other man showed them where the fuel was. It was behind the barn covered by hay bails; the tank was full to the top and had a large fuel pipe which stretched into the barn, they could pump the fuel by hand instead of starting the engine. By the time the fuel was pumped into the Challengers the tracks had been adjusted. Sgt Normal hadn't noticed that the day light had turned into darkness. Rota walked to wards the end of the barn. He could see a red glow far into the distance which made the night sky seem reddish in colour but at the same time it made the location safe in mind that they were not the ones that where getting the hammering. Rota turned and was about to walk back when the woman came over to him. Rota smiled at her giving a since of warmth towards her. He asked her what her name was; she replied that it was June. "June was an English name" said Rota, "indeed" June said. Her Mother was English but her Father was Germany, they had met many years ago and had decided to settle in the village once they married. Where are your parents now Rota wonted to know? June said that they had both been killed in a road accident three years ago and she had taken over running the farm as well as looking after her sisters. She seemed happy in talking about her family so Rota let her continue, before asking about the soldiers. He wonted to know if she had seen any bandages on the uniforms, June said "she noticed that they had a vehicle and a pipe type of style on their selves". Rota guessed that they were mechanised artillery unit which they had come across earlier. He went on to explain what they had done. June looked pleased and ran to tell the mayor.

While June and the other men were talking Lt Small approached Rota and said that they had better stop here for the night. Rota said it should be safe as they were now truly behind enemy lines and a long way off from finding our own lines. Lt Small continued in saying that the defensive line near to us would be the river Elbe, they should make for that.

June came back with smile on her face; she said the mayor was pleased in what we had done. He wonted to know if he and the village could be of any further help. Lt Small said "that they had done far too much in given us the fuel, and final asked if we could say here for the night". The mayor said "yes". Not long after June and the rest said there fare well and made their way back to the blood stained village. The drivers had finished the track bashing, now was the time for some thing to eat and a wash. The wash didn't go down to well with the lads; still it had to be done while they had a chance, it would wash way the story which they had all heard.

Rota said that they should leave at first light it gave the troop about ten hours to sort out the turrets and get the heads down. It was going to be a long day tomorrow. Rota thought hard about what he had been told and wounded what it was all about this carnage which was speeding through Europe at the cost of villages like this one.

Chapter Six

Half Tracked

Day five 29th August

Day break arrived far too early for Rota. He pulled down the zipper on his sleeping bag and made his way to the barn door he looked towards the sky which was mucky grey colour. Not the sort of weather you would have seen for a day in August. It dawned on Rota that the colour grey was caused by columns of smoke. Some one had been having a good prodding during the night. Rota turned and made his way back to wards his Challenger. He stopped short and gave her a quick once over. He knew that they would see more action in the days to follow and of the sorrow which would follow them until they had reached the safety of their own. Sgt Rota Normal was still looking at the challenger when Lt Small walked over. He handed out a fag and said "penny for them" Rota smiled and got out his lighter lighting his troop leaders first. Rota said "that he was thinking of what lay a head of us and what we had been told was it worth all this slaughter for a few barrels of oil. Lt Small drew hard on his fag before he answered and said "what has happen has happened, it for the like of this troop to stop it from happening again." Sgt Normal was stunned from these words which his troop leader had said he had never heard him speak like this before, he was growing up fast. But what he said was true.

Lt Small, lead the way from the barn and the village. Rota was at the rear, once he existed, the barn he turned his head slowly around and had a last look at the village, he noticed that smoke was still diffing from those houses which had been set alight in his heart he new that the village would never be the same again.

The troop move was going well they had covered plenty of distance from the village. Dave Tuesday was making a brew when Harry Young piped up "the troop leader had stopped". Rota had noticed. The troop leader came on the net and reported that contact

3 T80's plus 4 BMP's. Rota told Harry to swing hard right stick and to follow the dead ground to his left which would bring, them in dead ground to where the troop leader had given the contact. Cpl Jones did the left flanking in the end all three challenger had turret down position facing the contact they couldn't have planed it better if they had tried. Sgt Normal looking though his sights noticed that one of the T80s was stationery on its own the rest of the pack, were grouped together. Rota told Monty to lase the T80 the range came back at 1700 meters. Lt Small came on the troop net saying that they should take them out; Rota smiled to him self and thought here we go again more carnage would it ever end. Sgt Normal stamped out of his day dream he had a job to do and the survival of the troop. Rota said that he would take out the lone T80 the rest split between you and Cpl Jones. Lt Small came back and said fire on my command, Rota reported that he was ready, Staple had lased one of the other T80s and reported that he was ready. FIRE came over the net. The challengers rocked back on there suspension after letting go of the APFSDS it was a first round hit. Rota and Monty had already laid on one of the BMPs, before the first round had stuck home on the T80, boom another round hit, smoke was belling out though the barrel. Dave Tuesday kept loading until Rota said "stop loading". Looking though the sights both commander and gunner observed the after math of the disruption which they had done. The T80s were burning along with the BMPs not much was left not even body parts. Monty noticed that his first engagement had sent the turret roof flying sky wards and had landed up side down just like a frying pan. Monty traversed round and saw that the other vehicles were much the same. Cpl Jones finished of some of the crews with his COAX how they managed to get out the burning hulks was a miracle. Rota told Harry Young to reverse hard left stick away from the sight of blood and carnage. Once clear the troop formed up to lip frog to the next bound, they wonted to gain as much space as they could. After clearing the first bond Cpl Jones came on the net with the dreaded word CONTACT. An third T80 was in the tree line. Staple was board side on to him to late the first round hit Cpl Jones front right hand idler sending it flying along with the track. The T80s first round did the damaged he didn't get a second round off Monty had seen the engagement and soon put a round though

the drivers compartment sending part of the turret of in all directions he wouldn't be bothering the troop again. Lt Small soon came on the net informing the other two that further contacts where heading our way. Sgt Normal traversed right and noticed that it was a large convoy of soft skin vehicles along with BRDMs and tanks to many for two challengers to take on; only option was to sit it out and pray. Rota noticed a good location for a hide and told LT Small to follow him. Once they had found a suitable location Rota got on the net to Staple asking if they were all okay. Staple came back saying "that his driver had been hit in the head and was unconfused his gunner had a damage arm but was still able to fire the main armament" Rota told him to "depress is main armament and to switch of the main engine, open your hatches and look dead".

The troop didn't have long to wait. Sgt Normal noticed that one of the BRDM turned of from the rest of the column. He stopped short of the action which had just taken place a short while ago. Monty kept his sight glued to him; he noticed a slight movement on Cpl Jones barrel. The infantry then dismounted from the rear and started to move to Staples now broken challenger. They seemed to be making there way towards us and not the challenger, Rota said "that they were following our bloody tracks". The troop had about 3 minutes before they had to decided, to engage them. Out of the sky came a rush of thunder it was an American Thunderbolt A10 it didn't wait for a second run in it had finished of the entire column in one go. Once the smoke had cleared all three challengers commanders noticed that not a single vehicle had escaped the fire power of the A10. With the smoke still bellowing from the wreckage which lay before them Sgt Normal got on the troop net and told the Troop Ldr that he would go over and see what the damage was to Cpl Jones challenger.

Sgt Rota Normal crossed the open fields now littered with the dead he couldn't help but notice the carnage which lay before him. Rota observed the amount of body's which littered the corn field along with vehicle parts. The A10 had done its job. Cpl Jones climbed down from his challenge once he spotted Normal. Rota had a good look at Staple to make sure he was ok, he spotted blood on his right hand side of his face apart from that he seemed alright. Rota got closer and asked Staple "how was it". "Bloody rough", "you seem to come out of it alright apart from your face". "What about the rest of your crew" "The driver's bit out of it at the moment, but he should be okay soon, my gunner banged his arm on the breach, he said that he can still operate. "What about the loader" Staple said "he was fine". Sgt Normal and Cpl Jones moved to wards the right hand idler. The idler had been ripped clean off its bearing shaft along with track. Looking closely Rota noticed that the shaft witch housed the idler along with the roller bearings was in tacked, they were lucky. What this meant was that if they could find another idler they had the will and know—how, how to put a replacement back on. The only problem was finding one. Sgt Normal new they could not leave this crew to defend for them self's. They could put two on each of the rear decks of the remaining challengers, not very practical under the circumstances. Only option is two tow it. Rota told "Staple to get on the air and tell my crew to make their way down here". What are you planning to do"? "Am going to tow you all the way back home" said Rota. He gave them a promise before this conflict started that he would get them back home, that all so applied to the three challengers'.

Monty Kean brought Rota's challenger down and manoeuvred it to the front. Dave Tuesday climbed down and had a good look at the damage. Dave eyed his commander with a smile and nodded his head towards the idler indicating that it was a bloody mess. Rota said "to get the straight bar ready". Staple approached Rota and said "what about the track" Rota turned around after talking to Dave, then said "half track it". The crews worked like there was no tomorrow in getting the remaining track joined together. Once done they hitched up the two challengers together, first they had to remove the quill shaft so that the tracks would run feely. With the aide of Rota's challenger they managed to pull the Staples challenger forward so that they could insert the quill shaft tool in between the sprocket teeth. Now completed Staple would just follow Rota in what ever direction he would take. The damaged challenger still had it engines working, so it was still a fighting machine capable of inserting damage to any vehicle which might what to take on this troop of challengers.

While this was going on the Troop leader study his map ready for the next location. The light was fast going down before long it would be pitch darkness. They had to get a move on. Lt Small got on the net; he wonted to move in the next 30 minutes. Dave Tuesday said "that the Troop Ldr was on the net and wonted to know how long" Rota looked around him and said "10 minutes maximum "Dave relayed the message, the net was silenced again. Rota climbed abound his challenger giving it a pat. He new the next part of this survival would be slow but it had to be done what ever the cost. Rota told Dave "to inform the Troop LDR that they were ready." Lt Small came along the side of Rota and showed him were the next location would be. Sgt Normal figured it would be at least 50km drive. The troop was back on the move with the Troop Ldr leading. Rota looked behind him to make saw that Staple was okay, he was still attached witch as a good thing. Rota lowered his seat and lit up a fag, then placed his head against his sight griped his duplex and rotated the turret, he wonted one more look at the fallen, before the light faded.

The journey took for ever; well it did to Harry Young he was finding it hard going with a tow on. His beloved challenger was straining it needed a rest. The troop had no further engagement during the long road move. Sgt Normal noticed while he was traversing that there had been a battle of sorts. Monty piped up and said "do you see what I see" Sgt Normal looked through his commander's sight and noticed that Monty had laid on to a challenger amongst the carnage. Rota asked Monty if could make out its Call Sign. "It was Call Sign 11 from A Squadron", and it was one of theirs. Sgt Normal had a closer look and realised that both tracks had be blown of; its main barrel was lying forward over the drivers hatch. Rota his mind was racing ahead of him wondering if the idler was any good, and could they fix it to Staples challenger. Sgt Rota Normal plotted the grid reference down of the fallen challenger on to his map, one day when this carnage had finished they would come back to reclaim the dead.

Chapter Seven

A New Idler

Day Six 29th August

    The night hide the Troop Ldr had found was in the middle of rolling hills which stretched to both sides of the wood, they would be safe until the morning. Sgt Normal reversed Staple into a good firing position then dropped the tow. After finding a position for him self Rota dismounted and made his way over to Lt Small. He was met by Cpl Jones on the way. Lt Small looked over the shoulders of Rota and Staple towards the challenger. He gave the look that made Rota wounded if he was about the leave this call sign. Before he could give his views Rota said "did he notice the battle which had happened"? Lt Small said "he hadn't" Rota went on to explain his thought about taking of the idler in the morning then placing it on Cpl Jones challenger. Lt Small turned back to have another look at the befallen challenger. "Can it be done"? "We won't know until we give it try" said Rota. Okay Sgt Normal when shall you go. Frist light we give our self an emergency RV if the worst should happen. All three commanders study the maps and said the RV should be a good distance away.

    Sgt Normal walked back to his challenger; he noticed more fragments of the war imbedded with in the skirting plates. She looked worn and tried jut like me Rota thought. Dave Tuesday climbed down from the turret with a plate of beans and a cuppa and handed them to Rota. Sgt Normal looked at the orange beans on his plate, and then thanked Dave. Harry young was tightening the tracks with the help of Monty Kean, when Rota walked round the front of the challenger. "Now lads any problems I should know about?" Monty said "that he could do with a new track". Rota laughed and then went on to explain what they shall be doing in the morning. Harry Young looked at the rest of the crew before he said" I never have changed one before" Sgt Normal placed his hand on his shoulder to let him know that all shall be fine. Rota had done his fair share in idlers so it should be fine, they had the tools so what could go wrong.

First light was greeted by a fine drizzle when Rota removed him self from his sleeping bag. Rota lit a fag up then walked over to the nearest tree for a pee. Looking through the tree line Rota noticed that the drizzle had formed a haze which had nestled in the valley were the battle had be fought. Rota heard the rest of the crew moving about so he turned around and made his ay back. Rota told Harry Young to make saw that the tools were easy to get at, Harry nodded he had a mouth full of cold beans from the night before.

Sgt Normal quickly ran over to inform the Troop Leader that they ready. Lt Small told Rota that they would wait until midday. Sgt Normal ran back and placed one foot on the tow hook then gave the nod to Harry to crank over the main engine. Harry switched on the main battery switch then switched on the GUE on the GUE panel; he made saw that the GUE was on line before switching over to the main panel. Again Harry flicked the toggles switches down to start the main engine then pressed the starter button. The Roll Royce engine burst into life, he made saw that he made placed the engine on line. All warning lights had been extinguished Harry Young was ready to go. In the turret as soon as Harry Young had placed the GUE on line Monty Kean started his gun kit up. As soon as Monty heard the familiar sound he placed the toggle switch on so that the main barrel would travel with the movement of the body of the challenger. All systems were working. Dave Tuesday gave the Troop Leader a radio check. Rota settled into his commander's seat and placed on his crew helmet. Rota looked at the turret crew; they gave him the thumbs up sign. Sgt Normal spoke into his mic peace and told Harry to move forward. Once out side the wood Harry did a hard right stick in line with the edge of the wood. The haze was lifting which Rota had noticed early, it was going to be a hot day, and Rota could see the sun coming up in the far distance.

The distance to the carnage was soon covered. Rota pumped up his seat to look over his cupola what he saw was death and destruction of witch he hadn't witnessed before. The sight was followed by the smell of burning flesh, even thou it had been hours since the battle Rota could still smell the rotten corps of the dead.

Rota told Harry to pull over near the challenger, then to switch of the main engine. Harry Young flicked his switches silence befell the battle seen apart from the humming sound of the GUE. Harry slid back his drivers hatch then eased him self up. He too could smell the burning flash. Rota didn't waste any time in getting out the turret he grab his weapon then told Harry to clime out and to follow him. As soon as Rota had climbed out Monty moved up to his commander seat.

On the ground Rota moved around the befallen challenger, he was looking for the impact round which had knocked this Call Sign out. Harry called Rota over and said "serge I found it" Rota walked round to where Harry was standing. The round had entered the challenger just below the turret ring, forcing the drivers hatch to be blown off and at the same time it had lifted the turret from it mounting then it had settled down to ware it once belonged. Harry climbed aboard the challenger and picked into the drivers hatch what he saw was a mass of blood and bone along with human parts witch littered the driver's compartment. Rota had climbed up onto the turret; he noticed that the loaders hatch had been blown of along with the commander's hatch. The force of the round had caused a huge vacuum sending all three hatch's sky would. Rota looked in the loaders hatch, what he saw made him wont to throw up. Harry heard Rota cinching he looked up and said "okay serge" Rota wiped his mouth with his sleeve then waved his arm in a gesture to say that he was okay. Both Rota and Harry climbed down the challenger in silence.

Harry with tools at hand followed Rota to the right hand idler. Sgt Normal rocked the idler from side to side to make saw the roller bearings were okay, they seemed all right. Rota didn't hang about getting the idler off. It had taken them over two hours to complete. Rota and Harry carried it to the rear decks of his challenger, both Monty and Dave pulled it on board before climbing back into the turret. Cpl Jones still needed about 30 links of track. As both tracks had been blown of this made their job easy. Once Rota was satisfied he told Harry to clime back in and start up. Rota reversed Harry to were the track was lying. Rota made saw that the tow rope was firmly secure to the track and the rear tow bollard before climbing back into his commander's seat. After placing his crew helmet back on he told Harry to make his way back towards the troop. Harry moved of changing up the gears as he did so. Rota stood up in his seat then turned around to were the challenger was and gave a salute to the fallen. Rota eyes started to glow red with emotion.

On return to the hide Rota gave the Troop Leader a sit-rep of what they had seen. Lt Small was in silence while Rota explained the carnage which was in side the challenger. Once he had finished Lt Small reached into his side pocket and gave Rota a fag, he told his operator to throw out the brandy bottle. Rota smiled as he knew that the Troop Leader was much the same as he was.

The rest of the Troop was gathered around Rota challenger, Harry Young was telling all of them what they had seen. Rota came over and said "okay lads lets get this idler on" Sgt Normal watched as they carried the idler over to wards Staples challenger, his mind was with that challenger crew and what they had gone through. He hopped if his time was up it would be quick. Shaken his mind clear Sgt Normal moved of towards Staple. The idler was soon on. The challenger was in a well positioned which Rota had done as the troop had a clear path into which the new track could be laid. Once both tracks had been adjusted Sgt Normal told the driver to move forward and to pull both tillers to make saw that the idler was okay. Rota smiled to him self he had his troop back.

The day was fast approaching night fall. Sgt Normal noticed that dark clouds were blowing in from the west. Sgt Rota Normal wonted a word with Lt Small. He found him in conversation with his crew, it was good to se that that they had bonded well together. Rota said "that due to the falling light and the amount of work which the troop had done it would be best to stay a further night here then move of at first light". "It shall give the troop more time to short our self's out ready for the big push towards the Elbe River" Lt Small agreed. Cpl Jones came running up and said that he had re-adjusted the night stag. Sgt Rota Normal stag was at mid night, "time to get back into my sleeping bag thought Rota"

Chapter Eight

Warrior

Day seven 30th August

This conflict had now been ranging for six days. The Troop had covered 100s of kms and seen carnage that was only shown in the warmth of a cinema. Sgt Normal led the next phase which would take them nearer to the river Elbe. He new to survive the troop had cover as much ground as possible before the light restricted them in moving. They had the capability of moving at night but safety was first of Rota mind, he had a job to do and he would carry this out to the end. Dave Tuesday piped up and said "air movement is high" Rota looked to wards the clear sky, Dave was right the air movement was more active than it had been since the start of this. Sgt Normal told Dave "that he better close his loader hatch in case one should fall on top of him" Harry Young said "could he close his as he was cold" "Cart you take a joke then" said Monty. "Okay lads" said Sgt Normal just keep your eyes plead then. Dave handed a cuppa to his commander, "thanks Dave"

Sgt Normal twisted his neck to make saw Cpl Jones challenger was driving okay. His driver was toughing it all over the place, the idler was holding up. The troop had covered a good distance since first light all was going well until Monty Kean shouted CONTCT. Sgt Normal lowered his seat and placed his eyes firmly to his sight, what he observed were two Warriors engaging a BMP and a T80. Monty said "that they where hull down and giving it what for with there 30m radon Cannon" Rota got on the net to LT Small and gave him the grid of the contact and told him to act as FSG while Cpl Jones and himself sorted this out. Lt Small came back and said he was in position.

Cpl Jones took the left flank while Sgt Normal did the right. Both challengers took a turret up position, once ready they both opened fire. Monty witnessed his round hit the T80 just below the turret ring. He could imagine the effect that the APFSDS would have done once it penetrated the turret wall. Monty closed his eyes he had seen what he wonted to see. "Good shooting Monty" said Rota. Lt Small came on the net and informed both Call signs that no further contacts were in sight. Sgt Normal told Harry Young to reveries and, then goes hard right stick. Once clear of the small rise to his front Rota noticed that the warriors where still hull down unaware who had done the engagement. Rota told Monty to traverse rear this would indicate that the challenger was friendly forces. Dave Tuesday opened his hatch to let fresh air in after the engagement. The smell of cordite was lingering to the extent of causing headache. Harry Young piped up and said the crew were making movement; Rota pumped his seat up to get a better view. Okay Harry, pull over near the rear Call Sign. Harry slowed down and came to halt just behind the battered warrior; it looked like it had seen plenty of action. Sgt Normal climbed down followed by Dave Tuesday; both made their way to the rear door. The warrior rear door opened out stepped L/CPL Heater. Rota looked at him long and hard, then got out his fags and gave one to each of his crew before asking the question of what the hell are you doing here? L/CPL Heather spoke for a while telling Sgt Normal and Dave Tuesday, which they had been cut of from the rest of the section during a fire fight

The, day before. Both his Sgt and Troop Leader had been killed. It left him as the only NCO plus the other crew total of ten infantrymen. Rota asked if the radios were still working,

"L/CPL Heater said that they were" Dave Tuesday gave him the troop net frequencies. Sgt Normal wonted to know if both C/S where road worthy, L/CPL Heater nodded then entered the rear of the warrior to pass on the radio frequencies. Happy with that Rota told them to mount up and to follow him.

Sgt Normal brought the warriors to where the Troop Leader was and gave him a quick brief then suggested then make tracks.

Rota led the way followed by Cpl Jones then the warriors. Dave Tuesday gave both warriors a radio check, they were on the net. Sgt Normal noticed that the light was fading fast, he new that a small crops was about 10km away they should make it before the light faded for ever. Over the next rise Rota found what he was looking for, he informed the two warriors to leap frog him and make secure the crops to his front. No time was wasted. Rota watched through his sight in the actions of both crews, what he saw made him think that they knew what they were doing. L/CPL Heater came on the net informing the challengers that it was clear to enter. Rota was the last to enter the hide.

The challenger crews along with the warriors gathered in the middle. L/CPL Heater explained the circumstances which lead to the engagement early. It had started to go wrong when they bugged out from the first defensive position. His Troop Leader got the map grid reference wrong, which brought them, closer to the enemy instead of gaining a foot hold further to the Elbe River. The warriors first battle resulted in the Troop Leader being cut in half followed by the Troop Sgt the Crimson liquid spilled all over the turret running down towards the driver it was a sight which would turn the most harden. After witnessing the death of his Troop Leader L/CPL Heater managed to move the remaining warriors to a safe location, only to learn that they were truly lost. They managed to travel by day hopping that the direction they were traveling would take them nearer to the Elbe. Sgt Normal asked "what happed to the infantry"? L/CPL Heater took a deep breath before he gave the account of the senseless killing. All the infantry were dug in forward of the warriors. The T80'S with BRDM's came out of the morning mist, we didn't seen them coming until it was late. Two of the warriors where blown up with the first round, crews which were still in side didn't have a chance. L/CPL Heater witnessed along with his Troop Leader the slaughter of the men who were dug in, one was churned up by the tracks his arm was clearly seen going round the track before it was disgorged fallen in to the dirt which was covered by the bloody mass of human body's. The silence was an eerie place to stand and listen to. Dave Tuesday offered L/CPL Heater a fag he was grateful for the break. Sgt Normal wonted to know what sate of play the warriors where in. One warrior had been hit in the fuel tank but lucky for them the round went straight through, but had caused the warrior to run on one side of the fuel tanks. The remaining warrior had been hit just to the let of the driver's hatch, the round bouncing off, again they had been lucky. Lt Small took Rota by the arm and led him to one side. "Sounds a bit rough what they have been through" said Lt Small. Sgt Normal looked at the state of the warriors, he had made his mind up to that if they took both warriors with them then in due cause one would break down with lack of fuel. Only chance they had was to canalize it. Lt Small agreed.

Harry Young came up to L/CPL Heater and said "what's your first name then" L/CPL Heater turned round and looked at Harry and laughed its "Salt" "salt that's a funny name did your parents have a sense of humour then" Salt took a draw of his fag then said "Mum had a graving for fish and chips with lots of salt on them before I was born, hence the name.

Normal came back with the Troop Leader the look said it all. Cpl Jones looked at Rota he new that things were about to change. Lt Small informed the Troop that they shall take off what shall be useful to the remaining warrior, when that had been done Sgt Normal shall put an APFSDS round through it. Salt took his band of warriors with him to start, Harry Young and Dave Tuesday followed.

Rota walked to the forward edge of the wood. He could hear artillery fire in the far distance. His mind was racing forward he now new that if they had a chance at all in reaching the Elbe River they had to act like a fighting machine. Monty Kean walked up behind Rota with a plate containing a corn beef sandwich. "What wrong Serge" Rota didn't bother to look round he just said listen" Monty pined his ears back he could here the far distance rumble. "Theirs or ours" Rota chugged his shoulders, and then said "ours".

Chapter Nine

Ulta

Day Eight 30th August

L/CPL Heater led the way from the hide. Rota felt that being a smaller C/S and he had more movability and would be able to get out of trouble easier than the challenger. The sky was clear with a slight morning mist; we had a good distance to go so no time was wasted in putting the foot down and burning rubber.

Three hours from setting of L/CPL Heater came on the air CONTACT WAIT OUT. Salt reported that he had contact infantry dug in with a ZSU55 and BMPS. Lt Small decided that if we avoided this contact it would mean a further travel distance of some 50km decoy. The contact grid gave us a clear view of the enemy they were hold up in a slight ravine.

Sgt Normal suggested that two of the challenger act as FSG while the remaining challenger and warrior attacked front on. Rota used the dead ground as cover before getting into position. Rota told Harry Young to give him a hull down position. Monty looking though his sight noticed the tall antenna mast positioned in the centre. "Have you seen this Serge?" Rota reported the sighting back to LT Small it looked like a rear echelon set up. Lt Small counted 6 BMP, 3 ZSU55 with platoon strength of infantry. Sgt Normal came on the air and informed the troop that he would concentrate on the ZSU the remaining target's were free for all.

The first round from Rotas barrel hit the ZSU just short of the engine compartment; sending parts of the turret flying towards the blue-sky. Next target which Monty engaged saw the tracks blow off like it was made of match sticks. The crew trying to escape were mowed down by CO-AX fire cutting most of them in half; it was a blood bath for all of them. Rota saw that most of the infantry were trying to run towards the far distance wood land, L/CPL Heater saw them at the same time and opened up with his 30mm. Bits of body parts went flying in all directions they had no chance. With the last round fired came the utter silence of battle, it was over. Sgt Normal looked over towards L/CPL Heater his C/S had taken hits but seemed to be okay, "Salt make your way towards them and check for any survivors" "Roger wait out" came the reply. It was a tense moment before Salt came on the air. When he did he said that all was clear but they had found a live one.

Rota told Harry to move forward. LT Small and CPL Jones remained in the FSG. Dave Tuesday passed Rota's personnel weapon then climbed down towards were Salt was standing. Salt and his crew where gathered around the body on the grass which was covered in blood. "What you got then salt" said Rota. Salt turned around his face was looked drained, he just pointed. Lying on the grass was woman badly wounded. She had been hit in the left arm and leg just above the knee cap. Rota bent down, she was still alive but in a bad way. The bullet in the arm and leg had gone straight through but had taken a good deal of flesh and bone with it. Sgt Normal looked at Salt "we cart live her here, we'll patch her up and place her in the rear of the warrior" Two of the infantry had already ran back towards the warrior to fetch the stretcher. Sgt Normal left them to sort her out; he wonted to check what the command vehicle had been up too. Rota made his way to the vehicle, inside he found rolls of maps with position of the forward troops could come in handy thought Rota. He exited the vehicle then noticed that Salt and his crew where carry the woman back to his C/S. he ran to catch them up to make saw she was alright. Salt told Rota that she would be fine and no harm would come to her, "thanks" said Rota. "Once you re ready give me a call" okay serge. Sgt Normal climbed aboard his challenger, Monty wonted to know what they had found, Rota said "its a woman"; silence fell inside the turret apart from Harry who said "is she good lucking"? Rota turned towards Dave Tuesday and just lifted his head up in a jester of surprise.

L/CPL Heater came on the net and said they were ready. Rota informed his troop leader what they had found, LT Small was taken back that it was a woman also enquired if she was good looking. Rota said that she was okay in looks.

LT Small led the troop away from the now burning mace of vehicles, the Colum of smoke rising towards the havens. Rota was in the rear, looking back at the dead and the destruction it was a magical that any one had survived.

The next phase towards the night hide was travailed with out further contact. Lt Small found the troop a suitable location it wasn't far from the nearest hamlet they might have a doctor who could attend to the woman.

Chapter Ten

The Doctor

Day Eight 31ˢᵗ August

The hide was of a dense wood plenty of cover for all. Rota stayed in his turret for a long time before Monty, nudge his leg. Dave Tuesday was loaded up the vent tube magazines when CPL Jones popped his head in and said "the troop leader wonted to have a word with Sgt Normal" Rota looked over his cupola and nodded. He climbed down the slippery slop of the turret, stopping at the drivers hatch, banging with his foot to tell Harry to come out. The hatch slowly opened to relive Harry smoking a fag, he gave his commander a smile then eased him self out. "Not a bad day shooting" said Harry, Rota turned and smiled he knew he didn't mean any thing from his commits but sensed that he could use his words more apt.

CPL Jones ran over and joined Rota. Staple gave Rota a fag they both walked in silence towards the troop leaders' challenger. On the way Rota noticed that Salt had put a lien too up for the woman, he would go over once he had finished with LT Small.

Sgt Rota Normal gave an in depth report on what they had fond in the command vehicle showing the maps which he had retrieved. It looked like they were heading for the river. That made life difficult if they intended to cross it. Sgt Normal studying the location of the troops realised that their, was a small gap some distance further down the river, that had to be their crossing point. LT Small looked at Sgt Normal and Cpl Jones his eyes were suck with in the sockets his mind was racing ahead, he finally said "that its then we try and cross here" pointing at the village called "Legde". Lt Small asked how the woman was, Rota said that he would find out but she needs a doctor to short her injury's out if not then she wouldn't last long.

Sgt Normal walked towards the warrior, Salt and the crew were gathered around the woman again. When he reached them he found that she as talking to them in English. L/CPL Heater got up and walked a few steps towards Rota. "What's going on then" asked Rota. Salt said "that she had come round once we moved her" "Have you found out her name yet" "Ulta so she said" Rota made his way towards her and knelt down. Ulta eyes followed him, before he could speak Ulta said" you saved my life thank you" Rota looked at her and thought she was good looking, but wonted to know what she had been doing their. He began by asking what her job was. Ulta said that she was radio operator relaying forward information to the forward troops. Rota said that her name sounded German? Ulta went on to say that her mother was German and had moved to the Balkans many years ago and had married a teacher. "What made you join the army" "I had no choice all of us have to at one stage". Ulta started to moan at her injuries, Rota fetched the first aid box. Her dressing needs to be sorted out, but first he had to remove her clothing, Rota said "would she mind". Ulta looked into his eyes and said "no". Rota began by removing her shirt, he noticed that Ulta had no bra on and was taken back by the sight. It had been a while since he had seen such a sight. Salt handed Rota a towel to hid Ulta modesty. The wound was clean but it needs stiches to save infection from spreading. Rota bandage the wound as best he could before looking at Ulta wounded leg, witched looked a mess. Sgt Normal cut away her leggings to relive again her nudity. Rota looked towards her; her eyes said it all with out speaking. A blanket was fetched from the warrior and placed upon her naked body. The leg wound was in need of looking at by a doctor, a good portion of muscle and bone had been shot away. Once Rota had finished dressing the wounds, Rota asked Ulta how she became to be wearing what she was wearing. Ulta looked around the gathered troop; she started by telling them all that she wasn't ashamed of what she had done. "During the days before the engagement, my commanding officer decided that he fancied a bit of sport with me. I ran away but was caught and brought back to him. He slapped me around a bit then said he would teacher me a lesion which I wouldn't for get. He told his men to have a bit of fun with me first, they dragged me out from the command vehicle then proceeded to pull my clothing of me, before long I was naked being tossed around like a wag doll for their pleasure and torment. It wasn't long after that that the commanding office told his soldiers that he was ready for me". Rota interrupted Ulta and said "why they had picked on her" "It was because I was German and still a virgin". "Ulta went on to say that once they had entered the command vehicle", she stopped and said "that the rest you can imagine" "Once he had finished with me then it was the time for the soldiers to have there fun, that's when you started to open fire". "I ran and grab what clothing I cold find then went back in to the vehicle; my commanding officer was speaking on the radio telling them about you when I entered. He shouted to me to get out, I just stood there I noticed that his pistol was laying near by so I picked it up and then shot him at close range sending one round though his left eye which sent fragment of brains all over the place, the second bullet I aimed at his genitals and pulled the trigger until the pistol stopped working." "When I woke up I was here with you." Rota looked at the others then made eye contact at Ulta, "he said that they would look after her and no more harm would come her way" he had a small tear drop in the corner of his eyes which he soon wiped way, Rota didn't wont the rest of the troop to see that he was a worst. Salt brought Ulta something to eat along with a cuppa. Before Rota left Ulta she told them that a mechanised infantry unit was on it way towards the Elbe River, they where to RV with them in the next ten hours. Rota looked at his watch it had been 6 hours since they had the engagement. The radio message which the commander had sent would warn them that we were about, Rota hopped that they would not have seen the challengers, and time would tell if his presumption were right.

    Sgt Normal left Ulta and Salt; he found the troop leader talking to CPL Jones. He gave them a quick up concerning Ulta and what she had been through then told them about the mechanised. LT Small looked at the map and realised that they were near than they thought. Rota suggested that they should hold up here until things quite ion down. Sgt Normal went on to say that they should send recce party out to see if the could locate a doctor at he village. Lt Small looked at Cpl Jones, he nodded his approval. Rota was just about to walk away when the troop leader grab his arm. Rota sworn round and looked at him, "yes sir" said Rota. "Who do you wont to send on this recce" "Cpl Jones and the warrior infantry they should be okay in finding the doctor, Cpl Jones can speak a bit of German". Lt Small took a deep breath then said "okay warn him of". Normal found Staple eating a plate of strew. Rota explained the situation to Staple. "What time do you won't me to go" said Staple. Rota checked his watch again then said "in the next 30 minutes".

Cpl Jones gathered up his kit along with the rest of the infantry. He was given no more than three hours to find a doctor and return. The village lay about 5km away they had a full moon to guide them. Rota watched them go then climbed aboard Staple challenger and told his crew to keep an eye on them using TOGS. His crew were already looking through the system before Rota popped his head in. Rota looked at the crew and said "that he would be fine, make saw he has a cuppa when he gets back". Sgt Normal climbed on to the rear decks then jumped down and headed back to his own challenger, it was going to be a long 3 hours.

CPL Jones returned with the doctor in tow. He was met by Sgt Normal. Staple said that the doctor could speak English and was willing to help. All three of them walked over towards were Ulta was lying. She looked up when Rota approached her. The doctor said that he would have to stitch up her wounds but added that it would hurt; Ulta looked at Rota before she said "that she wonted Rota to be there" The doctor said that he could do with the help. Salt had gathered some 30mm ammo boxes together to act as a table. They gently lifted the stretcher and moved it on the boxes. When the doctor removed the blanket he could not help but notice that she was naked, he looked at Rota, and Rota said "it was a long story" They covered part of her body up exposing the part witch had to be operated on. The doctor injected the area around the wound to her arm first, this should numb it so you wont fell to much discomfort said the doctor. Ulta looked at Rota all the time that the stitching was taking place. Half an hour later the arm was bandage up. The doctor then examined the leg. He said" once he had finished she would have a slight limp" Ulta just gave a slight smile then differed of to sleep. Rota said "how bad was the leg" "I can try to save it but it will be touch and go" "She will be weak once she wakes up but she young and fit so she should make a full recovery" The operation took over an hour removing part of the damage tissue the bone had a slight chip from it but that should heal in time the muscle would be weak again that could be made stronger by exercise. Once the doctor had finished and had dressed the leg Ulta was placed back inside the warrior coved up with blankets, "she would be out for a few hours" said the doctor.

Rota and the doctor walked over to his challenger, he wonted to know why he had risked his life in saving this woman. The doctor said" That it was his duty to help the sick" "what about the reprisals if the Balkans found out "asked Rota. "They haven't come to our village yet if they do then I shall denied all of this waving his arms around the challengers" Rota placed his arm on his shoulder and thanked him. Cpl jones came over and said it was time to go; the doctor looked round and wished us good luck.

Cpl Jones took the doctor to the edge of the village, before saying good bye. Staple watched him walk away, turned then headed back to wards the hide. Half way back Cpl Jones along with the infantry heard gun fire coming from the direction of the village. They ran back towards where they had left the doctor. They managed to see him being carried of by a group of soldiers. Cpl Jones said he would creep forward to see what happened to him. It wasn't long before Cpl Jones witnessed the shooting of the doctor. He could see that the doctor was being questioned by the solders, one solder opened the doctors bag inside they found blood stained bandages. It looked like they wonted to know were they had come from, the doctor didn't give any thing away he risked his life to save ours. Staple gathered up the rest of the recce party and hurried back. The hide was on stand too due to the shooting. Lt Small came over to see Cpl Jones who explained what had happened. Sgt Normal came running over to find out what had happened, Staple looked at him and then said "sorry" The mechanised infantry where here. First light would be in about two hours they had time to get ready to move out. Rota said they would have a better chance if one of us held them back, while the rest of the troop got away. Before the troop leader said any thing Rota said "it would be his challenger that would say be hind". Lt Small didn't argue with him, he new that Sgt Normal had the best crew. All four commanders agreed that they should meet up at the next hide location which was about 50kms away from the village.

Rota hurried back to his challenger to tell them the good news, which wouldn't go to well with Monty. He found his crew at the rear of the challenger. "Ha serge what going on" Harry Young said. Rota said" the doctor had been shoot and that we would be acting as a rear guard action force so that the rest of the troop could get away." Monty piped up and said "he wonted a crew transfer" Dave Tuesday slapped him on the back then said "we couldn't do with out him" The crew laughed, Rota told them to be ready in the next hour. Sgt Normal studied his map for a long time before he told the rest of the crew what his plan was. Silence fell on the crew while Rota out lined his route, once he had finished Dave Tuesday said "what ammo should we use"? Sgt Normal said APFSDS, Dave nodded. Harry Young was going to say some thing but changed his mind; Monty gave him a glazing look. Harry looked at him then said "what" Monty just smiled then climbed aboard his challenger he wonted to make sure that his sights were clean and ready. Dave had a pee then ducked inside the turret, switched on the turret light looked around then started to rearrange his stowage. Sgt Normal lend against the front of the challenger fag in had, his thoughts else where. Lt Small creped up beside him, "all ready then Sgt Normal" Rota looked round "I should be if it all goes to plan, I cart see why it shouldn't" LT Small nodded then walked of towards his own challenger, time for them to move out. Lt Small uttered the word "good luck" turned and looked at Sgt Rota Normal he was going to need it.

The signal was given to start up. All three challengers roared into life, Rota watched as the other two challengers pulled out along with the warrior and Ulta. Rota gilded Harry out then told him to follow the edge of the wood until he told him to change. Sgt Normal lowed his commander seat then closed down. Dave Tuesday still half of his hatch open it was good to feel fresh air coming in. 2kms from the wood was the first location which rota had decided on. It made sense for them to travel down this track once they heard the sound of engines moving of. He didn't have long to wait, Monty gave the contact before Rota saw them. They came with lights on.

Leading vehicle was a T80 followed by BRDM, BMP, and what else they could throw at them.

Sgt Normal told Monty to wait until they had come round the corner. Silence and tension was felt with in the turret. FIRE shouted Sgt Normal Firing now; loaded Dave was quick to night thought Rota. Monty first round just bounced of the T80. Add 100 shouted Monty stop add 25 said Rota on shouted Monty Fire. Target, this time the round had lifted the turret clean of its mount what a sight seeing the turret flying like some up side down UFO. It came to land just short of the next vehicle in the column. Fire shouted Rota Fire Now shouted Monty, MISS FIRE shouted Monty, Rota looked through his sights another T80 was manoeuvring passed the stricken T80, Rota looked down at the breech block and noticed that the vent tube loader hadn't been rammed home, Rota yelled at Dave to ram home. It was two late the round from the T80 had stuck the right had wing send it over the turret and landing on the gear box decks. For fuck sake Monty finish the bastard of before he turns us into match wood. Monty didn't need telling again, he made saw his sight was lined up then he pressed the button boom the challenger rocked back and forward sending a puff of smoke out of the barrel. The round had done what it was made for; it had gone through the driver's compartment embedding up in the turret. Rota told harry to revise hard left stick, Monty kept his sight on the burning wreck by keeping his duplex pressed down this allowed the barrel to remain on the target while Harry was pulling either left or right stick. Once Rota had found his next location he told Harry to pull hard right stick this brought the front of the challenger facing the slaughter which had just taken place. They sat their and waited for the next phase. Dave made saw that the vent tube magazines were loaded plus he made saw that it was rammed home. Sgt Normal next target he noticed was a BTR-70 which had a 14.5mm gun fitted. It could do damage if given the chance. No mistakes this time said "Rota" Dave looked across the breech at Monty, Monty gave a smile. FIRE, LASING, FIRING NOW, Monty's round went through the commanders sight sending it in side then blowing of the rear doors followed by body after body. Rota told Harry to revise again, nothing REVISE HARRY, still nothing. Dave looked at Sgt Normal and said that his head set had come undone. Dave bent down under the barrel; he could see Harry but couldn't reach him so Dave nudges him with the spare CO-X barrel. Harry suddenly realised that his head set had come apart; fixing it he soon came back on the net. "Sorry Serge head set trouble" "Okay revises Harry and put your foot down. To late ping, ping; ping round after round came hurtle down on the turret. Damaged caused they would not know until later. While Harry was manoeuvring Rota noticed that the remaining vehicles had stopped. Two of the BMP'S had grouped together bad mistake, Monty lay on the front vehicle and fried. Monty had managed to hit the fuel tank sending up 100; s of meters of fuel into the morning sky, it wasn't long before it enlightened the glow you could see from miles away. The carnage had been done again. Normal looked to the rear watching the burring; Dave too opened his hatch to have a look. They could see burning bodies running and screaming, he gave Rota a looking glare then slowly descended back down in to the depths of the turret.

Chapter Eleven

Lost

Day Nine 01st September

    Lt Small could here the firing going on be hind him; he could all so see the glow of the fire Sgt Normal's plan had worked. He didn't waste any time in gaining distance between him the carnage that was going on in the distance. Passing the village Lt Small noticed that it was quite all movement was heading towards Sgt Normal. He looked over his shoulder to make saw that CPL Jones and L/CPL Heater were following him. L/CPL Heater warrior was bouncing all over the place, inside the infantry tried to keep Ulta from falling of the stretcher. The blanket's covering Ulta body were flung on the cold metal floor revelling her nakedness, the lads soon gathered up the blanket's and placed them back on her, this time they made saw they didn't fall of.

    Ulta woke up when they had replaced the blankets unaware what had happened. Ulta looked in pain; one of the lads reached over and gave her an injection of morphine which the doctor had left. In time she was feeling better and asked what was going on. The infantry explained what they had done and what Sgt Normal was doing. Ulta's face said it all she looked away from the lads and started to cry, she had fallen in love with this man who and saved her. A Europe which was at war had found love amongst the battle torn fields.

    Lt Small had missed the location of the grid given to him by Rota. He was ten kms further on. When Cpl Jones walked over to his challenger LT Small was lighting up a fag. "Were lost art we Sir" Lt Small blew out a long puff of smoke then said "he had missed the turn some kms back" "Cart we go back then" Lt Small looked at his watch, then he glazed towards the distance sky the light was turning to late to turn back now. "No we say here radio Sgt Normal of the new grid then wait." Cpl Jones walked back towards the warrior, he told the operator to give Sgt Normal a radio check. Salt was carrying out Ulta from the rear. She had managed to get a spare set of combat on to hide her modesty, she looked the part. Salt walked towards Staple. They both smiled at each other, Salt bent down and reached for his fags from his back pack before asking the question. "Well Staple what's going on" "the Troop Leader got us lost" "What shall Sgt Normal do if he can not find us"? Staple didn't have the answers but he hoped that Sgt Normal would eventually find us. He gave Salt a sung of his shoulder then walked back to his challenger. Before he left Salt operator came from the rear of the warrior, "no answer from Sgt Normal", "keep trying" said Staple.

Ulta eased her self up from the stretcher, she was felling better. She asked Salt what did It means that they could not get hold of Rota"? Salt bent down and sat with Ulta before looking at her then said "due to the distance that they had covered it was hard to gain a radio check with him, but we shall keep trying—don't worry okay" Ulta looked at Salt then brought her eyes towards the setting night sky and closed them in pray.

Chapter Twelve

Alone

Day Ten 02nd September

Sgt Normal wormed his way from the battle. Harry Young said "that he had a clunking sound coming form the right had track" Rota pumped his seat up then removed his head set to listen, Harry was right the sound could be heard for miles. He quickly looked at his map; Rota noticed a small crop just to the east of the village. It was a gamble being so near but it's the chance he and his crew had to take. "Harry head towards that crop on your right wing and put your foot down" "Okay Serge" Rota reversed Harry into the crops leaving the barrel forward. Harry switched of his main engine then waited until Monty had said the gun kit was of, silence again. All the crew listened for a long time, until Rota was satisfied that the cost was clear. Monty traversed of to check on the village using TOGS. All seemed okay at the moment. Harry quickly jumped down from his driver's compartment, what he found was the right hand wing plus the front skirting plate had been blown off. What was making the sound was the support arm for the skirting plate, twisted and bent it had lodge it self hull side to the track. Not a hard job if he could get the mounting bolt of. Harry climbed back on the challenger lined into the cupola hatch then told Rota what he had found. Sgt Normal looked up at Harry then across at Dave who was making a brew; "Harry needs a hand Dave" Dave looked at his brew, and then told Harry to grab his.

Monty was still looking at the village; he noticed moment heading to wards the main square of the village. Monty tapped Rota's leg, Rota replaced his head set "what up Monty" "have a look towards the village square" Rota placed his eyes firmly on his sight, what he saw was unbelievable. What was left of the mechanised infantry had turned up at the village and had gathered all its occiputs. Two soldiers carried what seemed to be part of a vehicle; Monty said "is the skirting plate".

The officer in charge started waving his arms about then struck a young man across the face sending him tumbling to the floor, he lay their until he was kicked by a second soldier. Rota's mind raced back to the telling of the story from the mayor and what had happened to them, it wasn't going to happen to this village. Dave climbed back in the turret and said that the arm had been removed. "Where's Harry now" said Rota "Having a pee" "Tell him to get back in his cab" Dave looked at Monty, he just nodded. Harry eased him self back in his driver's compartment, he tossed his fag butt out towards the front of the challenger. Harry made sure that his helmet was plugged in before placing it on his head, as soon as his ears were over the ear piece Harry heard his commander specking "Harry—Harry" "Sorry serge had to have a pee" "okay mate start up we're going to help the village". Rota went on to explain what he and Monty had seen. It was a while before Harry spoke again when he did his response was "let do it"

Dave loaded the main armament with APFSDS and made sure the CO-AX had a full box of 7.62, he was ready. Harry said that all systems where OK with him. Normal reversed his challenger to the rear of the wood. He wonted to make his way to the left of the village it would give them a better field of view. The challenger soon made the distance towards the hill which would give them a hull down position. Rota noticed that more soldiers had turned up along with two BRDM; s. The villages had gathered around the fallen young man who was still lying face down. Monty had sighted another vehicle to the right of the square a BMP, which made three. Sgt Normal decided to take out the lone BMP first then concentrate on the BRDM, s. Rota wonted to make sure that the village had all the help that they could give them so he decided to make challenger more visible. "Reverse Harry hard left stick, and then come up hull up to your right facing the village" "What serge did you say hull up" "Yes Harry just get on with it" Dave and Monty looked at each other while the challenger was reversing, "Dave placed his finger to his head indicating that he thought the serge had gone of one"

Monty just laughed, then he placed his eyes firmly to his sight, his fingers where on his duplex controller ready to switch from main argument to co-ax. Harry brought the challenger slowly to the crest of the hill.

Sgt Normal laid his sight on the lone BMP, "on reported Monty" FIRE—LASING FIRING NOW boom the challenger rocked slowly on its tracks with the hand break fully applied she didn't more back much. The round lifted the BPM firmly of its wheels; it came down with a thump knocking road wheel stations clean off. It wasn't long before the fuel tank exploded sending columns of burring fuel sky wards. Rota noticed that the solider commanding turned his head slowly to wards where the challenger had fired from. It was his last look, he was cut in half by a burst of CO-AX, and part of his body was throne in both directions. Rota told Monty to take out the two remaining BRDM, s they had started to moving away from the main square. "Loaded shouted Dave" FIRE, LASING FIRING NOW, Monty had taken out the furthest vehicle with a direct hit just below the turret. The turret along with it crew was hurtled towards the main square. The second vehicle had stopped; back mistake Monty again had turned this vehicle into a burring wreck. Sgt Normal told Mont to switch to CO-AX; he didn't won't any solider left. Looking through his sight at the target which Monty as engaging Rota noticed that most of the soldiers had been cut down with round after round hitting it was a blood bath. Once the engagement had finished and the smoke which had started to clear Rota saw that the village people had started to clear away the dead, what happen to the wounded Rota didn't what to think about. Satisfied that the work had been done Rota told Harry to reverse. "Where to serge "asked Harry? Sgt Normal looked be hide him before answering Harry they had left the village in a state of carnage, but hoped that they had saved more than would have been put to death. Rota told Harry to head for the far distance wood line.

Dave Tuesday tried the radio again, still no contact with the rest of the troop. Sgt Normal gathered that the troop had got lost, but new that they would be okay. It wasn't long before harry said that they had reached the wood line. Rota moved the challenger up and down the side of the wood looking for the perfect place to hind. Once he found it he reversed the challenger gun front. Cam net was soon placed in front BV was on sentry was posted it was like being on exercise. Monty Kean was first on stag he had done well today, then again his shooting never let the crew down, thought Rota. For the rest of the crew Dave was shorting out his turret, Harry needed to adjust his tracks. As for Sgt Normal he made his way to the edge of the wood, he needed to be alone for a while he had a lot of thinking to do.

When Rota returned Harry had made a list out of the damage. The challenger was missing two skirting plates support arm a front right had wing both head light and a number of cupola sights, and neuromas bullet marks peppered the challenger from front to back. Dave looked gloomy when Rota entered the turret, "what wrong Dave" asked Rota. Dave looked up to where Rota was sitting and handed him the ammo state. Rota took out his fag packet and lit up a fag before reading the list, the list wasn't very good reading. Dave had counted that the challenger was down to its bear minimum of main armaments rounds 10 APFSDS rounds, 15 HESH rounds and 8 boxes of 7.62 rounds. Rota placed the list in his pocket, looked at Dave then said "it be okay we haven't got far to go now" Harry popped his head in, he had finished the tracks. "Just in time Harry food up mate" Harry squeezed in the turret with Dave, and then closed the loaders hatch before switching on the turret lights. The food was good; they had plenty of tin food to last for a few more days. All three ate the food in silence; Rota was the first to finish and then handed his mess tin to Dave. "I take Monty's out" Dave plated up Monty corn beef stew. Rota reached over and placed it on his cupola. He grabs his map case and weapon and preceded to clime out the turret, the sky was dark, darker than he had seen it before. Sgt Normal followed the wire which led to where Monty was, "food up mate" Monty looked around he moved over to make room. "Dark sky to night" said Rota, Monty looked up with a mouth full of stew then just nodded. "I'll take over you get your head down, tell Dave to relive me in two hours" "Okay sarge"

Sgt Normal had been on stag for about 45minute when he heard movement coming from his front. He placed the head set to his ear and warned the rest of the crew to stand too. Dave Tuesday new the emergency RV. The movement grow louder as it was approaching,

Rota could make out two figures. He waited and waited until they were right upon him. Rota stood up, shocked to see that they were to elderly men. Both men raised their hands. One of the men could speck English; he explained that they had escaped from the village before the shooting had started, and where trying to make their way to his daughters' village which was about 10km to the south east. Sgt normal told the men to lower there hands, he got on the head set and told Dave what was going on. Rota waited until Harry came out to relive him. Harry turned up looked at the men then entered the sentry post, he wasn't happy he hadn't got his head down.

The two men followed Rota to wards the challenger, once there one of the men stopped and looked hard at the challenger before Rota asked what the problem was. It turned out that they had seen two more of these plus a small one heading to wards the village of his daughter. At least Rota new they had made it. Dave climbed down from the turret with two cups of coffee; both the old men looked up when Dave handed the drinks over, they were glad of a hot drink. Rota let them finish there drink before asking them if the village had any fuel which they could have. The elderly man who could speak English said that his daughter was a framer and was bond to have fuel for them. Rota wonted to know how far the village was, and could they find during the night. Both men looked at each other, the one who couldn't speak English kept pointing to wards the challenger. Eventually they walked towards Rota and told him that the distance could be made during the night but it would be slow. Sgt Normal gathered his crew around him he wonted to make them aware what might lay before them. Monty, Dave and Harry smiled then said" we have come this far lets do it now"

The none speaking German entered the glum of the challenger's turret he was Surprised how big the interior could seem from the out side like a bloody cathedral; especially when it was all in darkness. He could just see the dim outline of one of the crew weapons in its clips on the other side of the compartment. It seemed a hundred yards away too far the other end of a long tunnel. Normal placed his foot on his commander's seat, this too looked small to be real, thought the old man. The old man friend then placed his footing on to the loaders seat ready to direct Sgt Rota Normal and his crew. The old man standing behind the breach block watched with amassment how? this large barrel kept moving in unisons with the motion of the challenger. Dave Tuesday had only one spare set of head phones witch he handed to the old man who would gilding them. Dave kept an eye on the man inside the turret, he smiled at him given him an assurance that they would soon reach the safety of the farm soon.

Harry Young drove opened up he could see better going through the wood, just look up to wards the sky so that you can see the tops of the trees there you have a clear view of the tracks a head. Rota told him to slow down as he was throwing the old man about. The journey seemed to last for a long time. It wasn't long before the villager said that they would be clear of the wood soon, what lay a head was open field at the far distance stood his daughters village surrounded by trees and a major road route. Normal halted the challenger at the for ward edge of the wood. Mounty scanned the village nothing was sighted though the TOGS. Rota looked at the old man, then said "you can walk from here to make saw the village is safe" Rota looked at his watch then added "that if they did not return in an hour then we would travel on" The old man related this to his friend" They both said they would be back soon. Monty watched them cross the open field they were making good time for oldies thought Monty. Harry Young eased himself out his cab, climbed on the turret and popped his head in side the turret. Dave was busy sorting out the ammo for the CO-AX. Harry turned his head towards his commander; he had his head firmly fixed to his sights. Not wonting to disturb his boss he made his way to the gear box and slowly lifted one of the decks. The heat was felt on his face which warmed him. Harry eased him self down and placed his feet on the steering disc, it felt good. Dave Tuesday lowed the turret dimmer lights then looked out side, he noticed Harry sitting on the gear box and told Rota. Normal took his eyes away from the sight and pumped his seat up and spoke into his mic telling Dave to keep an eye on him.

Sgt Rota Normal checked his watch; it was all most an hour since the old men had gone. "Any sighting of them Monty" "No nothing yet" Rota told Dave to get Harry back in his cab, it was time to move. Once Harry was settled, Rota told him to start up. Monty said "That they had movement coming towards them" "Can you make them out Monty" "Yes it's the old men" Both villages came strolling in as if they were on an evening stroll. One villager climbed aboard the cold armour of the challenger. He told Rota that it was safe to enter the village; his daughter's farm was to the far right of the village as you looked at it. A signal barn light would be switched on when you got near. Normal told Harry to ease forward at a slow speed and to head to the right of the village. A signal light had been switched on when the daughter heard the sound of the challenger approach her, Harry pulled his tillers to make for the barn doors. Once inside the doors where closed behind them. Normal told Harry that he could turn of both engines. Silence was golden for a brief minute before the old man said that the fuel pump was ready. Dave and Harry soon filled the almost empty tanks, they certainly wonted it.

The old man was talking to his daughter when Rota approached them. He told them that they should be done soon. The old man said that they could say as long as they felt it safe to do so. Normal thanked them then took the old man to one side and whispered in his ear. The old man smiled then walked to his daughter, she looked at Rota then smiled a few moments later she came back with a bag wrapped up with string and handed it to Rota. Normal looked in her eyes she seemed to know that the parcel she gave him was for a person he had fallen in love with, she placed her arm on his and gave a tight squeeze. Harry came over and said the challenger was ready. Normal thanked them again for their help, turned around a boarded his challenger once more. The sound of the engines echoed though the barn. The two old men along with the daughter watched the challenger head of into the darkness of war. Normal raised his arm in salute until the darkness adsorbed their view.

"Where to asked Harry" Rota had already pin ported a location which would take them closer to the rest of the troop, "hard right stick Harry and just keep going"

Chapter Thirteen

The Reunion

Day Ten 03rd September

Day break broke so came the sound of artillery fire witch was heard in the not to far distance. After they had left the barn Rota had taken the crew a further 20km away. The night location was sold wood land. It was time to catch up with the troop. Dave Tuesday gave the Tpr Leader a radio check—still nothing. "Okay Harry creep for ward to the edge" Harry selected first gear, the 70 tonne challenger eased of her hand break and slowly moved across the open space. The view at the edge of the wood was clear. Rota looked at his map then looked at the ground in front of him. Normal noticed smoke coming from the direction of where he wonted to go, he told harry to head for it but to use dead ground all the way.

The ground was smooth going, the sun was out it was going to be a bright day, thought Normal. Harry dropped down to forth gear them creped to a hull down position before Monty said that he could see. Harry selected revise gear. Monty and Rota eyes fixed to each sight couldn't believe what they witnessed. Directly to there front was the troop.

What they saw was a T72 accompanied by BRDMS engaging them on both flanks. The challengers were hull down but still they where getting a hit by light flank from the BRDMs. Monty had laid on to the T80 and lased the target it had come back at 1500 meters. Dave had loaded HESH he was ready. FIRE—LASING FIRING NOW shouted Monty. The round projected it self to wards the turret of the T72 Monty saw it explode just for ward of the commander sight. The sight along with commander's hatch was flung to one side relieving the inside of the turret. Monty could see the gunner trying to escape from now the burning T72. The T72 unlike the challenger did not use loaders in their tanks, they had automatic-loading guns so they only had three men in a tank crew, but their system had a weakness. If the automatic-loading system failed, then their tanks became useless. No more would this tank see action again. Monty opened up using his CO-AX to finish the gunner of, the driver tried in vane to open his hatch he would die a slow horrible death being burnt a live. Normal switched the turret to the BRDMS who had grouped together, Dave reported loaded. FIRE—LASING—FIRE NOW shouted Monty again the challenger rocked back and forth on her suspension before the round stuck home. The nearest BRDM had been lifted of it wheels coming down to earth with a thump, its back doors being flunk open in a desperate more to escape the carnage. The other BRDMs tried desperately to avoid the engagement, they didn't get far. Cpl Jones finished one of sending a column of smoke and ammo hurtling sky wards.

Sgt Rota Normal reversed his challenger away from the hull down position, making dead ground to his right he soon came to where the troop was and signalled the troop Leader to follow him.

Normal took his troop to a safe location ready for the night. All three challengers Looked good amongst the shadows of the trees. Harry was the first out, running towards the other two challengers. Rota climbed on top of the turret he wonted to see Ulta. Cpl Staple Jones walked over to Rota challenger. He climbed on to the rear decks and shook Rota by the hand. Staple told Rota that the troop Leader had followed the wrong route. Normal said that they had been seen by to old men, if it wasn't for them tell us where you had gone we would have never have found you. Normal reached in to his pockets to make saw the parcel was still their, it was. Both Staple and Rota dismounted from the challenger and walked over to the Tpr Leader.

Salt Heater had posted the sentry's out while the crews gathered round for bit of banter; it was good to see the troop as one again. Normal was talking to Lt Small when Monty Kean nudge his arm, Rota turned around to see Ulta walking with the, add of a makeshift walking stick. She had come along way since her operation thought Normal. Ulta eyes where full of joy in seeing Rota again. When she got closer Normal walked over to wards her. He placed his arms around her and squeezed her gently; he could feel her harden nipples through her combats. Ulta started to cry, and then whispered "I love you". Rota let go of the squeeze then handed her the parcel. Ulta looked down at the brown paper tied up with string; she gently untied the parcel to revel a par of kickers. Ulta just burst into laughter gazing at the objects. "How? Did you manage to get these?" Rota went on to say that he came across this old man who had helped us out, plus he had a young daughter. Ulta whispered in his ear "do you won't me to put one par on or do you prefer the commando sly "? Normal didn't have an answer, his eyes said it all. They hugged again followed by a kiss; Rota told her that he would not leave again. Normal asked how her leg and arm was, Ulta said that she still had pain but was able to walk better and stand for longer it was heeling nicely.

    Rota left Ulta with his crew then gave Lt Small an up date since they had left each other. Sgt Rota Normal mentioned that he thought that they had got of a radio message before he had time to finish them off, if so then all eyes would be out looking for us. Lt Small reached over and op-ed his map indicating where they were and the village of Legde. It ranged about 100km way a far distance when you are being hunted. Just then Cpl Jones turned up with a list of the ammo state, it didn't read very good. The troop of challengers were down to it bear minimum, given each challenger just 8 APFSDS, 10 HESH AND 4 BOXES OF 7.62. Salt and his crew had 30 APDS, 20 HESH. Normal said "we make the Elbe River in four or five days" "what about the fuel state" "if we keep to the roads we should make it" Lt Small looked at his commanders, it was his call. "Okay we shall keep to the roads, move out at first light" Rota said "that he would get a route together"

    Sgt Rota Normal slowly walked back to his challenger on the way he passed the warrior, Ulta as sitting on an ammo box talking to the crew. He would see her in a minute Rota wonted to check on the sentry's post. Normal found them just short of the wood line. The clear sky was turning dark and cold, rain clouds were forming up, and it looked like it could rain. The sentry's asked Rota if he was okay, Normal handed them a fag but said to keep the light down, "thanks sarge". Rota turned and headed back to find Ulta. Ulta smiled when she saw him coming she was so happy, and looked stunning. Ulta handed Rota a cuppa, and said that she had managed to put a par on when know one was looking, they were a good fit. Ulta face turned from a being happy to that of a person who had the world upon her shoulders. "What wrong" Ulta looked hard at Rota then said" I won't to ride with you from now on" Normal looked over to his challenger he new that they didn't have the room for her; she could not stand for hours on end with her injured leg. His gaze turned towards her and finally said "okay" Ulta flung her arms around him then went inside the warrior to fetch her belongings which wasn't a lot. Salt looked at Normal then just shrugged his shoulders.

Dave Tuesday was in the turret when Ulta climbed aboard, "knock, knock" said Ulta. Dave looked up he smiled knowing that she would be staying with the crew from this moment on.

Chapter Fourteen

Death of the Warrior

Day Ten 04th September

    As Normal un—zipped his sleeping bag he felt the dampness of the morning air. It had rained for most of the night, sending droplet of rain running though his cupola sights. Rota switched on the dimmer lights of his turret and leant his head back against the rest of the breach block. He reached out and touched the cold steel of the turret with his fingertips. It was cold, damp with the condensation of the morning rain. She was a good tank, reliable, responsive to the treatment she received from his crew. Rota was told long ago that he remembered being told how it had been when the cavalry regiments lost their horses before the start of World War Two, men has wept as their mounts had been led away to be replaced by armoured vehicles. If the situation were reversed, Rota thought, he would have identical feelings; you get to know a vehicle, trust it, and understand its likes and dislikes. Rota had never owned a horse, but millions of pounds worth of challenger took some beating. The womb like darkness and security of the challenger fighting compartment was comforting. Normal was shacking back to life when Dave popped his head in the turret. "Switch the BV on sarge" Normal turned the BV on using battery power, had one more look at the turret then eased him self out through the loaders hatch to be greeted by a warm smile from Ulta. Ulta had stayed close to Rota all though the night, sleeping with him on the rear decks feeling the warmth of the gear box against her all most naked body; she had managed to slip her combat trousers of for the first time since she was found lying amongst the dead and the carnage a few days before. The show of her kickers to Rota had been the high light of the night before she pulled the zipper, of her sleeping bag slowly up around her neck. Ulta slipped her combat trousers on in the comfort of the sleeping bag, before Dave pulled away the challenger vehicle sheet which had kept most of the rain of the her and Rota. Mounty had climbed in the turret though the cupola he was keen to make sure his sights were clean ready for the road move. Harry Young walked around his challenger making sure all was secure. Sgt Rota Normal made his way to the rest of the troop. L/CPL Salt stopped him mid way asking if he could bring in the sentry's, Rota checked his watch then said "okay Heater bring them in and make sure they have a cuppa and a bite to eat" Salt smiled and nodded. Lt Small was cleaning his teeth when Rota got to his challenger, "morning sir" Lt Small looked up after spiting out a mouth full of tooth paste mixed with water. Lt Small's driver came running up to Sgt Normal he had a look of dismay on his face. "What wrong mate" Just checked our fuel am down to all most fresh air" Lt Small turned around and couldn't believe what he had just heard. "Don't worry sir we shall find some soon" then walked of to find his own crew; time was all most up to pull out.

While Rota was walking back his mind was fast forwarding to think how far behind the rear echelon was in catching up with the advance guard. Rota new that the advance guard would be running out of fuel soon, they had to have a replen of some sort.

Dave Tuesday was standing on the loaders step when Rota climbed aboard his challenger, Harry was making sure that his head set was plugged in, he presumed that Monty was in his seat waiting to switch on the gun kit. Ulta was standing forward of the beach loading the CO-AX, she looked the part with her head set on. Ulta smiled when Rota sat in his commander's seat placing on his own head set. Sgt Rota Normal spoke in the mic making sure all the crew could here

Lt Small came on the net to tell each call sign to start up; Rota would lead the road move. Lt Small would bring up the rear. Once they had exited the hide the rain had stopped, all crew's would drive opened up. The sun had started to break though the morning clouds which warmed Rota, he shivered with the warmth. Sgt Normal lowered his seat to check on Ulta; Dave had moved his loaders seat along the turret rail for her to sit on. Ulta looked across the vase distance to wear Rota was seating he seemed such a long way away, unable to touch him due to the breach block moving up and down in motion with the main body of the challenger. Rota gave her the thumb up sign Ulta responded in blowing him a kiss, Monty had a quick glance across at Dave before turning his head to his sights. Three hours into the road move, Lt Small came on the troop net informing Sgt Normal and the troop that a Colum of smoke was about four clicks behind them heading in their direction. Rota quickly pumped up his seat and twisted his neck to look rear; he reached behind his seat for his binoculars' what he saw was a Colum of soft kin vehicles in the middle was a fuel tanker. Sgt Normal looked at his map; he noticed a sharp bend coming up, on each side was a steep incline unsuited for wheel vehicles. Rota decided that the best option was to ambush this Colum in the middle of this.

    Monty kept his sights firmly on the leading vehicle; it wasn't unlike the Land rover which he was used to drive in. Sgt Rota Normal gave the order to open up with CO-AX. LASING—FIRING NOW shouted Monty. The first burst was aimed at the driver and his passenger. Monty witnessed the rounds hitting the driver in the left shoulder which ripped the arm away from the rest of the body. The driver franticly tried to keep the vehicle on the road. His rear passengers jumped out only to be crushed by the on coming vehicle. One was flung on top of the bonnet only to fall under the rolling tiers which crushed his legs to a plume, blood was flying all over the windscreen the driver unable to see brought his vehicle head on to the side of the forward vehicle, which by now had crashed diagonally across the road stopping any vehicle from passing. Both the driver and passenger where flung out though the windscreen only to be cut down by Monty's rate of fire. No one survived this CO-AX onslaught. The Fuel tanker had stopped both solders running for there lives only to be stopped by Staples gunner. Further down the Colum the carnage was much the same as it was from the front. Lt Small engaged the rear vehicle packed with troops, one solder a woman was cut down her shirt being flung open by the shear volume of bullet which had entered her body. Smoke was bellowing out from the now wreaked vehicle's which had been scatted all long the road. Sgt Normal radio L/CPL Heater to move forward. Salt came on the net informing the troop leader that the fuel tanker was intact. Lt Small didn't waste any time in manoeuvring forward to the tanker, he soon had it working. All call sign's filled up Rota was the last he only needed a top up. Once he was finished Rota took the troop faraway from the Aftermath of what had taken place. Sgt Rota Normal guessed they had been lucky he had a dreadful felling that the troop luck was about to run out.

Rota lead the troop cross country before re-joining the road again. Lt Small decided that L/CP Heater would take the lead, once they had pulled over into the small copes. Sgt Normal checked to make sure the area was clear before calling forward the rest of the troop. All call signs switched of there engines silence as golden again for only a sort paste of time. Rota let Monty climbed out, he watched as he did so next was Dave from the depth of the turret followed shortly by Ulta, Dave helped her out. Ulta looked tried and worn out, Rota noticed that her wound to her leg had started to weep. Ulta took her time to climb down from the front of the challenger, Rota was waiting with the first add box. Ulta looked in to his eyes; love was beaming though those, Rota too had falling in love. Sgt Rota Normal helped Ulta to the side of the challenger he had to re-dress the wound which meant that Ulta again had to revel he new knickers, she felt the warmth of the exhaust out let against her body as she lend backwards it felt good. Rota soon dressed the wound which looked like it was heeling well apart from the small weep. Ulta flung her arms around Rota's neck and drew her lips close to his; both embraced with a passionate kiss which lasted long until Monty Kean interrupted to say that the troop leader wonted to see him. Ulta let go of her arms and watched Rota turned and walked to the rear of the challenger. Monty came towards Ulta and said that "Dave had made her a cuppa" Ulta placed her arm though his and they both walked away to find Dave.

Sgt Normal found the other commanders gathered around the front of the Troop leader's challenger. All where studying the map when Rota walked up. Lt Small greeted Rota with a warm smile, and offered him a cigarette. The next phase took the troop over a bridge which the troop leader was worried about. Sgt Normal looked at the rest of the commanders then said" send the warrior in first it small and quick than the challenger" LT Small glanced at L/CPL

Heater, Salt turned to wards Staple who nodded. "Okay sir what do you wont me to do"? Lt Small out lined the plain he would send Salt out first followed by Staple, me then Sgt Normal who would at as FSG, move out in 30 minutes. Rota was walking back to his challenger when Salt came running up towards him. "Sarge how's Ulta?" Rota said that "he had to redress her leg apart from that she is fine" "Tell her we miss her on the warrior "Sgt Rota Normal said he would. Rota watched him go then shouted out "take care Salt" Salt turned and raised his arm in acknowledgment.

Sgt Normal reaching his challenger noticed his crew gathered around the front. "Okay lads what's going on" Harry said "that they had lost a road wheel station" "which one" "it's the inner one on the right had said, third station" Rota walked round, all the rubber had gone, and the outer wasn't looking to good either. "Have you tightened the nuts up Harry?" "Yer"

Rota told his crew what the plain of action was prior to crossing the bridge. Sgt Rota Normal looked at Ulta and asked if she be okay, she can go with Salt crew if her leg was hurting. Ulta took it in turns to look at each of Rota crew then finally looked at Rota, "this is my crew now" she said. Sgt Normal told them all to be ready to move in ten minutes. Both Harry and Dave helped Ulta aboard; Rota was the last to climb aboard the challenger. Inside the fighting compartment all the turret crew were busy prepping for the next move, Ulta was reloading the CO-AX she had learnt the drill well since Dave Tuesday had shown her what to do, and this left Dave to load the main armament Quicker. Monty was waiting to start the gun kit; fingers paused on the gun control toggle. Slowly Rota placed his crew helmet on his head static came though the ear piece, only to be broken by the voice of the troop leader telling all call signs to start up. Harry Young didn't need to be told; he placed his finger on the starter button on the GUE panel and waited for the sound which told him the GUE had started, he quickly made Shaw that the GUE was on line before starting the main engine, he was ready. Sgt Rota Normal watched the troop move out before telling Harry to move forward. Rota moved cautiously forward, avoiding the sky line and working his way to wards the road.

It wasn't long before Salt gave the contact report of the bridge; it was time that Rota made his way to the FSG. Best speed! "Step on it Harry" he ordered, and felt the challenger surge forward, bucking over the road surface as the roar of the Roll Royce engines increased. Sound was always relative to discomfort in a tank, he thought wryly. The only good thing was you didn't hear most of the noises of battle. It was still there, though not far in front of him. Rota pulled of the road much of the low hill had been scalped by artillery fire, but there was some protection close beneath the limestone outcrops. Rota near the top paused and looked back towards the troop who was creeping forward. L/CPL Salt Heater advanced slowly traversing right and left. His front part of the warrior had only jutted on the bridge when it happened. The first round was a direct hit on Salt and his gunner; they didn't stand a chance, the 30mm Radon Cannon was still firing when it was hurtled though the air along with the turret. Rota saw Salt, trying in vine to get out of his turret how he had managed not being killed was any body's guess, he was dead it was the hope that Rota was hopping for which never happened. The driver was killed by the second round ripping the hatch and part of his body with it. Sgt Rota Normal looked though his sights as the rear door was flung open, he counted one, and two, three, and then four no more escaped the inferno of the warrior. The two that didn't manage to get free died an anguishing death by fire, the survivors only managed to crawl to the ditch near the bridge only to be cut to pieces. Rota had seen the flash of the T80 barrel, Monty laid on it, APFSDS, was loaded. FIRE—LASING FIRING NOW. The challenger's armour had stuck home, sending part of the turret falling to the ground. Sgt Rota Normal pushed himself upright in the turret and gazed through the episcope. The sky was bright with fire and the searing trails of projectiles flying through the air towards there targets, the ground pocked by explosions that briefly illuminated drifting clouds of smoke. Rota wonted to help the infantry with prophylactic fire using the challengers CO-AX, he was to late the bank of earth ahead of his challenger was hurled aside. The concussion of the explosion knocked Harry Young backwards from his driver's sight, his head smashing backwards on to the retaining head rest only to be rocked forward to his sight. Ulta was shouting through the intercom, wonting to know what had happened Rota herd her shout he looked over the breach block as the main armament rocked back wards sending another round at the target. "its Salt his dead" Ulta turned her gaze to the CO-AX placing another box of 7.62 on the now empty weapon, her eyes full of tears sending small droplets of water on to the belt fed machine gun. Ulta's mind was racing backwards to the time they had spent together it seemed only a few moments in time since they were together haggled up in the warrior now they have gone.

Sgt Rota Normal told Harry to reverse before the next round found its mark. Lt Small engaged the second T80 sending a ball of fire through the air, pay back time had been complete. Cpl Staple Jones manoeuvred his challenger to a hull down position he had Seen, the third T80 surrounded by the tree line. The T80 had all so seen his movement; his round found it mark sending a round through Staple gear box lifting the decks clean of its hinges exposing what was left of the now static challenger. Fundable to a second round Staple tried in vine to move. Rota had seen the explosion he didn't need to witness a second destruction of the troop. Sgt Rota Normal laid his turret on and pressed his firing backer button on his duplex control sending the APFSDS flying through the air towards the now exposed target. The round hit the target below the turret ring, in slow motion Rota saw the tank being lifted a few feet from the ground before falling back on its tracks, no exposition was herd no smoke just a motionless target furlong in the world of carnage.

The smoke differed away revelling the battle seen, and Salt warrior. It lay alone with the turret pointing the way home where it had falling. Silence befell the turret of Rota's challenger. Rota new he had to act soon and save the rest of the troop. Sgt Rota Normal got on the troop next and called Staple, it took a while before Staple answered when he did he sounded far away. All his crew had been spared they had been lucky. His challenger looked a mess this time Rota new it couldn't fixed with out a new gear box. Lt Small was the closest to L/CPL Jones he didn't waste any time in closing the distance from where he was. Smoke was bellowing out from the rear decks of the challenger, Lt Small could see the extent of the damage caused by the T80 round, if it had been aimed at the turret then Staple and his turret crew would have been blown to pieces. The troop Leader heard the sound of Rota's challenger; he slowly turned away from the disruptions to watch Sgt Rota Normal gild his challenger towards the warrior. When Sgt Normal reached the seen he found it un-foamingly to the carnage which he had already witnessed before, this time it as different as these fallen comrades where mates who had gone through hell and back just so that they could reach the safety of the Elbe River. L/CPL Salt Heater's body was still lying inside his turret when Rota approached, as he had seen when the turret had exploded from the body of the warrior. Looking at Salt one would think that he was asleep; he had no wounds to speak of. Rota gently removed his dog tags then realised that the bottom part of his body was missing; he turned around just in time to see Ulta coming to wards him. Rota climbed down from the turret and walked to her, holding the tags in his left hand which were dangling in slow monition of his walk. Ulta stopped and looked down at the dog tags, Rota followed her gaze then lifted his eyes to hers they where full of tears. Sgt Rota Normal placed his arms around her neck and slowly brought her close before saying "take these Salt would wont you to have them" Ulta opened her hand out to clasp the dog tags, once they were placed in her palm Ulta tighten her fingers around them then walked back to the challenger. Rota watched her climbed aboard he turned one more time to gaze at Salt and his crew. He noticed that the sun had gone behind the cloud making the carnage dark and ere place to be. Once aboard Dave and Monty looked at him with sadness. Rota "uttered the words to his crew that from now on no one else shall fall to this sinless quest for oil". Harry Young turned his challenger around and made his way to the other two.

Lt Small had put the tow on they were ready to move when the challenger had reached them. Sgt Normal climbed down and ran over to LT Small to give him a quick brief on Salt and his crew. Lt Small listed with out any interruption until he had finished, his 50 gazed looked past the shoulder of Rota at the smouldering warrior, and he nodded then climbed aboard his own challenger deep in his own thoughts of what had happen.

All three challenger's drove passed the fallen warrior paying the complement of a salute to the fallen. Rota followed in the rear, before he reached the warrior he told Monty to traverse of right then dip his barrel it was the only honourable thing he could do in paying his and the crew of the challenger there respect.

Chapter Fifteen

The Pound

Day Eleven 5th September

Sgt Rota Normal sat with his back against his back rest and closed his eyes for a few moments in time. His mind racing back to the last engagement wondering if he could have done any thing different in preventing the death of Salt and his crew. Rota's conclusion was no, the tactics were right for that road move what happened, happened. Harry Young was speaking on the crew head set when Rota came back from his day dream; he was saying to Dave that the troop leader was burning white smoke. Sgt Normal pumped his seat up as far as it would go, before he could see the troop leader's challenger. Both exhaust where laying a dust cloud of smoke which could be seen for miles, Rota quickly got on the troop net telling the Tpr Leader to pull of the road and head for the large copes to his right. Trailing smoke all the way they managed to get all three challengers into the dense woodland. Rota was the last in making saw the challenger tracks had been covered. Lt Small had reversed CPL Jones deep into the heart of the wood; the moon was casting shadows though the trees with its golden autumn leaves stated about the ground. Smoke was still bellowing out from the troop Leaders challenger when the engine where switched of, quickly Staple Jones placed the vehicle sheet over the rear decks this seemed to dampen the smoke. What damage had been done by towing the challenger the troop would have to wait until the morning to find out?

Sgt Normal eased him self out of his cupola, he stood on the NBC pack looking at the troop and noticing the smoke rising through the vehicle sheet. Rota looked up to the sky it was getting dark, with a full moon to add to the light of the wood. It looked a peaceful place to be broken only by the distance rumble of artillery fire. Dave Tuesday was the next out the turret followed by Ulta, she looked tried. Ulta stood by the side of Rota, before Monty climbed out to join them. In silence Monty handed the cigarettes out to Rota and Dave, the silence was interrupted by shouts coming from the depth of the turret it was Harry Young. Dave Tuesday climbed down the turret to Harrys drivers hatch, it was stuck fast. A round from the T80 which had landed short of the challenger had thrown up a piece of shrapnel and had bedded it self in to the rim of the hatch. Dave went back and told Rota what had happed. All four looked at each other before decide ding if they should let Harry out. With the aide of the crow bar the hatch was eased open to revile Harry puffing away on a cigarette. Rota along with Ulta and the crew had a good laugh it broke the tension of the days engagement. Due to damage to his hatch Harry would have drive open up from now on.

 Lt Small came over to see what all the laugher was about, he soon joined in when Dave Tuesday told him what been going on. Sgt Normal took the troop Leader away towards Staple Jones challenger they wonted to see the extent of the damage. Climbing aboard the challenger the first thing they noticed was the amount of oil which was laying about the rear decks. It was a mess which had to be cleaned up before they could see any thing. Lucky for the troop they had entered a wood which had a small pond deep in the middle of the wood which might pervade stand of sorts.

 Both Rota and Lt Small jumped down from the challenger walking away they both turned and studied the extent of which the troop was in, out of the three challengers Rotas was the only one which was fit for action. "What shall we do" asked Lt Small. Sgt Normal answered "wait until the morning we have been through a lot to day nothing can be sorted out until then" Lt Small looked down towards his feet moving the leaves with his boots like a lost child who had lost a toy. Rota placed his arm around him and said "it be okay sir" then slowly walked of to find the sentry's. CPL Jones had sent out his gunner and driver for the first stag. Rota noticed that they had demounted the commanders GPMG when he reached them. "Hi sarge any news of the damage to the troop leaders wagon" Rota told them it was to dark to see things should look better in the morning. Satisfied that the hide was secure the best that they could, Sgt Normal turned around and made his way back to his own challenger. Reaching the centre of the hide Rota could tell that things had got back to normal the way the troop was doing things with out the aide of Salt and his crew. Harry Young walked over to Rota telling him that the challenger was fit for roll, but they had lost another road wheel rubber, same side as the others. Monty had traversed rear the first time in a long time. Harry Young with the help from Dave Tuesday opened the rear decks checking each dip stick. For a challenger which had been on the go since the out break of war she was in a very good state.

There was a sense of isolation making the men even more nervous. They were now totally cut off from the NATO armies; a small island, encompassed by an ocean. The war had swept past them, friends must have already died but as yet they had seen more action than any one. Sgt Normal gathered his thoughts and climbed aboard his challenger, he new the next few days would be tough for all of them he had to keep going. Ulta was all most out the turret clasping a towel under her arm, when Rota reached her. "Where you of then" Ulta looked at him with eyes which said come and find out. "I am off for a swim" Both Monty and Dave looked at each other the look that makes soldiers the way they are. Rota smiled and watched her climbed down the turret to the ground, then head of towards the pond.

While Ulta was away the crew carried on with task in making saw the challenger was fit. Dave Tuesday reorganised the turret the best he could, what ammo he had left was placed in the ammo racks near the radios for easy use. Dave collected the empty 7.62mm rounds from the spent case sack and lifted it up towards Monty. Sgt Normal had said to burrier it which they did. Once the decks had been lowed Monty traversed front, the challenger was ready again for what ever carnage lay in front of them.

Ulta had walked to the centre of the wood to the clearing; the sun had almost gone casting its last shadow upon the still water of the inviting pond. Ulta slowly un-did her combat shirt button by button, she puled the jacket out of her trousers to revel her toned body. Ulta let the shirt fall from her body, her nipples

Harding in the cool of the evening. She raised her arms trying to reach the stars which lifted her breast to there full round ness. She clasped her arms around her neck to release the tension of being cramped inside the challenger's turret. Ulta draped her arms to her Brest feeling her Hardened nipples pinching them and creasing before she started to undo her trousers. Once the final button was undone the trousers fell loosely towards the ground showing her full fruitful body. Ulta stepped out a leg at a time in a sexual movement, turned and looked at the clear inviting pound before slowly removing her kickers. Ulta slowly then walked to the edge of the pound before taking the plunge to submerge her body. She surfaced in the centre of the pound swimming like a mermaid. She felt the bottom of the pound with her feet witch came up to her middle. The feel of the water against her body made her feel sexy, she turned on her back floating and looking at the full moon which was peaking through the trees trying to get a view of her, her nipples perturbing above the water, the motion of the pond drifting slowly over them. She raised her hips to bring her triangle of black pubic hair above the water; Ulta placed her arms between her open legs feeling her inner sexual pleasure which had roused her since entering the pound. Her sexual pleasure with moans of joy where puff led by the gently movement of the water cascading between her legs and across her body, making waves that reached the banks of the pound. Exerting the pound Ulta dried her body then laid down naked letting the warm air of the night wrap it self around her. Placing her clothing back on Ulta made her way back to Rota and the crew, not before having a last look at the pound whispering a thank you. With a warm smile on her face she left the pound and the secret behind her.

Chapter Sixteen

The Fog Bank

Day Twelve 6th September

    The sun was creeping above the rolling hills casting a fog bank across the lowlands when Sgt Normal climbed out though his turret he had been on the last stag. Placing the BV on he looked at the troop though the morning fog, he thought that the place looked like any other which he had been to on exercise. A cracking sound came though the head set it was Monty giving his commander a radio check, all was quite as it had been though the night. Lt Small climbed aboard making his way to see Rota. "Morning Sir" "Morning Rota" it had been the first time the troop leader had addressed him by his christen name. Sgt Normal offered him a cuppa which he took. "Its going to be a warm day" said Lt Small looking though the fog glaring at the sun breaking though. Rota looked up at the sun and then turned towards the Troop Leaders challenger and pointed. "What's the damaged sir" "My driver said it's a spit coolant pipe coming of the header tank. "Take the one from Cpl Jones to replace it; he won't need it for a while" laughed Rota. Lt Small said, had he seen the damage done to Staples challenger, Rota turned his gaze towards the other challenger and said "NO" Ulta by now had climbed aboard to be with Rota; Lt Small smiled at her then looked at Rota with the look that said he was a lucky bloke.

    Dave Tuesday started with the breakfast while Rota made his way to see Staple; he was interested in what the damage was. Staple's crew had cleared all the oil away from the rear decks and had left them open. The damage was by far worst than Rota expected, the round had ripped the fly wheel away from the main engine not only had the round knocked out the gear box it had damaged the main engine. Both fan belt pulleys and tensioners had been blown off along with the part of the right had fan blades. The round had gone though exiting after bouncing off the bank of oil filters at the far side of the hull. Look had it that it had not penetrated the fuel tanks. Staple said that the GUE was still working witch meant that they still had the capability of using the main armament. Lt Smalls' driver appeared carrying the damage coolant pipe. It didn't take him long to replace the pipe the damage one was replaced on Staples challenger tapped up with rag.

Sgt Rota Normal walked over to see Lt Small he was studying the map when Rota caught up with him. "All set sir" said Rota. Lt Small looked at the map then said "I make it we should be at the Elbe River in about two days from now" "okay sir I shall lead be ready in 10 minutes then"? Lt Small checked his watch it was all most 07.30am, then nodded.

Rota ran over to Staple to tell him we are moving out in ten. Sgt Normal walked back to his own challenger, only to stop to have a look at the troop which he had bought together as a fighting troop. Harry Young was in his cab waiting to start up; Rota gave him the signal to Crack over the engines. The sound was deafening in the stillness of the wood echoing though the trees, the exhaust smoke diffing towards the morning haze.

Before Rota climbed in to his own commander's seat, Rota heard the familiar sound of Monty starting his gun kit. Placing on his head set Rota looked across the vast empty space of the turret towards Ulta, she had tied her hair back before placing the head set on. He had wondered why she had that bright smile on her face once she had come back from the pond he didn't ask it was her secret he would find out one day.

Creeping forward to the edge of the wood Harry Young manoeuvred the challenger between the autumn trees rolling over the fallen leaves towards the clearing which would take them further to the Elbe River and home. The fog was still lying with in the dead ground which offered them a slight protection against the might of the oppressing forces. Rota turned his body to see Lt Small emerge though the cleaning towing Staples challenger; it would make a fine photo if he had a camera with him.

The troop had cleared the fog bank at the next rise; to the right of them laid the road and safety. It was when the troop Leader had cleared the rise that they came under small arms fire, 14.5mm rounds from a BTR. All three turrets traversed off and started lying down CO-AX fire along the ridge line. Bullets from the CO-AX went flying in all directions sending up columns of earth before they found their targets. The targets soon came under a barrage of fire power sending parts of the vehicles flying along with human parts witnessed by Monty looking through his sights, smoke started to rise to wards the morning sky. Unknown to the troop a lone T80 was getting into position ready to engage the leading challenger which was Sgt Rota Normal. Just then the optic sight from the T80 glistened in the morning light which Monty had witnessed with out orders from his commander Monty traversed his main armament towards the target and shouted "ON" Rota looking through his sight quickly saw the T80 before Monty squeezed his firing breaker switch to release the APFSDS to wards the target. As the gunner hit the firing button and the propulsion charge detonated in the breech. With the Roll Royce engine screaming the roar of the gun was impressive within the confines of the fighting compartment. The challenger heaved upwards with the shock a direct hit above the drivers hatch sending another turret flying though the air only to come down to earth like a falling piece of broken metal. There was a heavy clank of mental from the vertically sliding breech block as Dave Tuesday reloaded, and a mist of cordite smoke swirled inside the hull; most of the fumes were exhausted outside the challenger, but some always drifted back. Tuesday shouted "Loaded" Another T80 appeared further along the ridge it was like running the gauntlet. The only chance the troop had was to put the foot down and go for it. The T80 position where they were had the disadvantaged as they had to fire down hill. Sgt Normal informed the troop to make the best speed to the far distance tree line. Cpl Jones swinging his turret to the left and right letting rip his main armament. Rota could see the effect it had on the toe once he fired the recoil seemed to bring the challenger back wards in slow motion. Monty Kean fired another round at the second T80 this time it fell short. The T80 was quick of the mark to send around at Rota challenger, the round landed to the left of the right had track sending up fragment of dirt and mental. There was a heavy blow on the side of the challengers turret witch sent a violent shockwave through the fighting compartment and rang the mental of the hull as though it were a vast bell obscuring both sights until the air cleared. Staple had seen the action and had sent his last APFSDS round hurtling towards the waiting T80. His round found the mark ending the life of those that were inside. The ground was rising more sharply, smashed woodland laid ahead, stumps of distorted trees, pitted earth, gaunt roots. A thin hedge ran diagonally across the landscape to the left, party destroyed, the bushes torn and scattered they had made it, but at what cost to the troop. Rota lead the battered troop to the next hide which hid them from the on sauté which they still had to engage. Once inside the safety of the wood could the extent of the fragment of metal be witnessed?

The smoke was still rising from the carnage which had just taken place. With the safety of the wood Sgt Rota Normal quickly climbed from the turret, followed by Monty Kean. Ulta was next to exit the turret; she had a slight blood stain on her injured leg Rota observed, Ulta looked down to were Rota was looking. Dave Tuesday passed out the first aid box to Sgt Normal who helped Ulta down to the side of the challenger. "It got to be dressed, pull them down Ulta" said Rota. Ulta looked at Rota before she undid her combat trousers, letting them fall to the ground like she had done at the pond. The wound wasn't that bad considering what Ulta had gone though. Rota quickly redressed the wound not before the troop leader came round the side of the challenger to witness Ulta standing with her trousers around her ankles wearing only her skimpy kickers. Lt Small turned his gaze from Ulta while she made her self presentable. Ulta smiled at the thought of some else looking at her body. Rota realising that Ulta was looking at some one turned towards the troop leader and smiled. "All done" said Rota. Lt Small turned his gaze back to Sgt Normal. "What wrong sir" asked Rota? "Cpl Jones challenger has taken a ponding, the14.5mm rounds ripped of his gear box decks along with the long tool box" "Can he still be towed?" Lt Small scratched his head he was a worried man Rota witnessed, "He should be okay but we cart take more of what we have been though". "I know I have been thinking that as we are so near the Elbe we should keep going though the night" Lt Small placed his hands in his pocket to bring out a tissue, blowing his noise he looked at the state of Sgt Normal challenger he too had taken a pounding. "Okay we shall do what you fell is the best" Sgt Normal said that they should gather the troop together and explain what we are going to do.

The troop gathered around the troop leader's challenger, they all had been though hell and back and now so close to home all they wonted was to get their. First off all the state of the ammo had to be addressed. Staple had 3 HESH, Lt Small 4 HESH, 4 APFSDS, Sgt Normal; challenger had 5 HESH 6 APFSDS. Lt Small looked at each of his troop before saying that the Elbe River was in striking distance, Sgt Normal and my self have decided that we should push on through the night. The troop was silent before Monty Kean piped up and said "what about the ammo state we cart afford to engaged another forces which we have just uncounted" Sgt Normal turned to look at Monty and the rest of the troop he new that Monty was right. "We can not afford to say here until the war has ended we have no option but to push on regardless" The mood lightened somewhat of what Rota had said. Dave Tuesday smiled humourlessly. "He could be right still we're not dead yet are we". The troop smiled united by the signal most powerful human emotion there is. The will to live. Or more aptly, to survive. Men didn't live in this war; the way they lived could not be called living. They existed. They lived and fought like animals. Some because they wanted to, others because they had to or, like the men of this troop, because it was the only way they knew how.

Sgt Rota Normal along with his crew made there way back to the challenger. All five of them stopped short to have a close look at the damage the challenger had had to bear. She was in a right state to look at, most of her skirting plates had been blown away, along with both front wings guarding the idlers. The challenger had 40% of the road rubber missing from the road wheels. All rubber pads on the tracks had gone, the right hand exhaust out let had been torn away by small arms fire, but still she kept on going in what ever Rota asked of her. The challenger had half the camouflage paint had been burnt off. The challenger looked like a candidate for the breakers yard. Harry Young went forward on his own his tank was in need of some tack adjustment. Harry placed the ratchet on the idler adjuster and stated to pump. Dave and Monty climbed aboard to sort out the turret stowing what little ammo they had for easy loading, the last of the vent tube rounds where loaded into the magazine, no spare vent tubes no mistakes. The water which was in the header tank was the only water the challenger had left, food consisted of a can of beans; strew steak, processed peas, sausages and a tin of jam marmalade.

They still had plenty of coffee and tea, along with the beer which they brought aboard from Honhne. Monty Kean stood on the loaders step with the beer in hand, he whistled in the direction of Rota and Ulta who looked up to where Monty was standing. Ulta held Rota's hand looked in to his eyes then said "fancy a beer then". Rota smiled it had been a while since the last time they all had one. Ulta lead the way to the side of the challenger, his crew were waiting with ice cold beer which had been kept in the bag charge containers. Rota smiled and then said "cheers" "Cheers sarge" "You better keep it low lads don't let the troop leader see you" Harry Young came from the rear of the challenger and said "it be okay sarge the troop leader and Cpl Jones are doing the same" Ulta was the first to laugh out loud followed by the rest of the crew, it broke the tension which the crew were feeling, the next few days would see the troop being torn apart before they finally crossed that bridge to safety, if they made it.

    Lt Small came over with beer in hand he wonted to see Sgt Normal alone. Both walked to the edge of the wood deep in thought. Rota stated by saying that they should pull out before last light which was in the 3 hours time. Lt Small wonted to know what the chances where for the troop. Rota kept his gaze to the front before answering, "If we stick together then we have a good chance of getting though" Neither of them new that what lay ahead of them was a company of artillery supported bay T80, BTR70 and BRDM-2. Lt Small still was not happy about traveling at night even thou he had told the troop that he was, Rota told him that most of the enemy had leapfrogged pasted them. Before they went back to their challengers both men shook hands, with out saying a word.

    Rota returned to find the crew sitting with backs against the remaining skirting plate still drinking the cold beer. It worked out that each of them had three beers each, nothing that would stop them carrying out the drills of the challenger tank. Rota joined them sitting next to Ulta. "When do we move out" Ulta said. All eyes turned to wards Sgt Normal who was having the last drink of the beer, he placed his eye to the bottle neck to check it was empty before looking at the crew and then finally said "3hours from now" Monty stood up then made his way to the nearest tree, not bothering to hide what he was about to do, Ulta had seen it all since joining Rota and his crew so going for a pee was nothing new for her.

Ulta steadily stood up then reached for the hand of Rota, he looked up to the out stretched hand before placing his hand in hers. Both walked away from the crew, it was their time and moment for both of them to have a few quite times, together. They both walked from prying eyes to the far side of the wood, strange that war was all around them and yet for these precious moments the war could wait. Locked in each others arms surrounded by the trees they passionately kissed for a long time. Rota could feel Ulta's tender nipples through her shirt how he longed to have her, once this war had finished he would take her away. Ulta broke away from the kiss looked deep into Rotas eyes and then asked "will we make it" "we shall, I wont let any thing happen to you that I promise" Tears started to form in the corner of Ulta eyes her feeling's where that great to wards Rota, she could not bear anything to happen to him, she new deep down that he would go out of his way to safe guard the troop if it meant that his own life had to end. Ulta had the comfort of knowing that if Rota had to satisfice his life then hers would end with him. Before they returned to the challenger and the waiting crew, Ulta and Rota shared one more embraced together. Slowly and with each other in their own thought they climbed aboard the challenger. Sgt Normal was the last to enter the turret; he turned to see LT Small looking at him before he entered the confines of his cupola. Monty had switched on his CCPU ready for the TOGS system to be lighted up. With a light hiss of the TOGS door being opened the system was ready; the twilight was brought to life again. Monty said it was clear to the front; a chill went down Rota back before he told Harry Young to pull forward.

All three challengers emerged from the depths of the wood. The evening sky was clear with a full moon to shine the way home. Each challenger turret swivelled from side to side in a quest to find a target, none was found. The only sound which was heard was broken by the throbbing sound of the tracks along the road.

Chapter Seventeen

Empty Village

Day Thirteen 07th September

Sgt Rota Normal observed the burning hulk through his sights, a fieriest fight had left the carnage for others to witness. Rota could make out the commanders limp body hanging half in and out of his cupola. His smouldering head was still sending up columns of smoke diffing high to the waiting night sky. The barrel lying, if in a furlong posture in a deadly salute to the dead. Sgt Normal lowered his gaze from his sight and looked through the gloom of the turret. Dave Tuesday was peering through his loaders sight his safety guard made safe, Ulta laid slumped her hands acting as a pillow resting on the movement of the CO-AX, the moon casting a showed on her slender body. Monty Kean eyes glued to his sight traversing his barrel from left to right, finger paused on his selector switch ready to fire the next round, oblivion to what was going on. Rota new that Harry Young was driving opened up. He seemed far away from the rest of the crew, in a world which was his until it changed with command from his commander.

Silence was broken by the troop Leader on the net telling both challengers that a small village was around the next bend. Sgt Normal had all so noticed the village. He quickly told both challengers to stop while he moved closer to the unfamiliar sight which he saw through his sights. The TOGS system didn't revile any heat sauce in any of the brick houses; it was a village of the dammed. Creeping forward in low gear Harry made his way through the centre of the village, he looked up to the open windows the curtains blowing in and out. Not a sound or movement was seen, the village was empty. Lt Small was getting inpatient in the wait for Rota to come on the air. Sgt Normal eased his challenger to the far side of the village before calling up the rest of the troop. Lt Small came along with his tow he crept through the deserted village until he found Sgt Normal standing up in his cupola. Rota looked behind him when he heard the challengers approaching, collocating his webbing Rota climbed down the front of his challenger and made his way back wards to the others. Lt Small lifted one of his head set ear pieces from his ear and listed to what Rota had to say. Sgt Normal informed him that his driver was finding it hard to pull his left stick; it had to be sorted out. The village acted as a good location to carry this out. Harry Young eased him self out of his cab, carrying the spanner which would undo the bleed nipple on each of the steering callipers Harry made his way to the rear of the challenger stopping at the loader hatch and tapped Dave on the head, "give us a hand mate" said Harry before lifting up the rear gear box decks, the heat hit him full in the face sending a shiver down his back at the same time sending warmth to the part of his body which needed it. The steering reservoir was empty. Harry made his way back to the turret to let Sgt Normal know. It would take time to bleed the system with the help from Dave Tuesday.

Ulta, standing half out the turret, watched the night sky towards the west. Flashes of distant light flicked like summer lightning along the horizon, and the sky itself was coloured as though it reflected the illumination of a vast city. It was almost beautiful, smoke clouds glowing scarlet, violet and a continuous pyrotechnic aurora borealis shimmering above the village and surrounding fields. She was feeling alert, self-confident; it had been far more of a Strain on her nerves while they waited for the steering to be done. Ulta found it hard to believe that this was war, though there was plenty of evidence. Every small village or even farmhouse they had passed had been destroyed, tumbled and blackened stone walling, crazily-angled window frames, fallen roofs, deserted . . . . still smoking. Wrecked vehicles, some unidentifiable, others which looked as though they had simply been abandoned, littered open fields. There were bodies, corpses lying awkwardly in the wreckage; a line of uniformed men arrayed beside a hedge, neat and tidy as though ready for inspection, weapons beside them, the night hiding the bloodstains and the wounds. Shell and rocket craters, dark irregular patterns in the fields; shattered tarmac and cobbles, sewer pipes and drains, burnt woodland lay around this vast world in which we live in, would we ever see piece again. Rota heard the distance sound of Dave and Harry telling each other to pump or hold back the steering tiller, one side had been done it had taken what seemed like hours but reality was it had taken no more than a few minutes to complete. Harry crept forward to wards the cupola, Sgt Normal was looking at his watch he thought it had stopped the hands slowly going round as if the hands were making there own world of time, oblivion to what was going around them secure in there own place in history. Harry Young informed Sgt Normal that the steering had been done but the steering pads where almost down to the metal, Rota looked at Harry then said "not much further to go Harry, try to avoid to much hard steering" Harry had a quick look around him looking at what lay in every direction trying to understand his commanders last comet, he shrugged his shoulders then made his way down to the safety of his drivers compartment, feeling safe amongst the intermit space of the challenger. Dave Tuesday closed the gear box decks and waited until Ulta had descended into the glum of the turret, before she entered Ulta reached out and touched Rota arm, Rota looked hard into her eyes he new that what lay a head might be the end of his challenger and crew, he broke a small smile of reassurance before Ulta had disappeared.

Dave Tuesday broke the sound of the crackling on the net by telling the troop leader that they were ready to carry on. Harry eased the challenger for ward to the far distance line of homes which marked the end of the village.

The delay meant that the troop after it had passed the village would soon be traveling in day light. The morning haze of the day was breaking though; the distance to the Elbe River was getting nearer. The morning light reviled smoke rising in the direction of the river. To the left bank was a small crop which the troop could hide. Sgt Rota Normal told Harry Young to head direct to the crop. Once inside the confinement of the wood Rota eased his challenger to the very forward edge of the clearing, what he saw made his hairs on the back of his neck stand up. Lt Small with Cpl Jones on tow pulled up not to far from Rota's own challenger. Both Lt Small and Cpl Jones climbed down and ran towards Rota's challenger.

Chapter Eighteen

Elbe River

Day Fourteen 08th September

There was a sense of isolation making the commanders even more nervous. They realised for the first time that they were totally cut of from the rest of the battle group, a small island, encompassed by an ocean lay before them. The Elbe River with it solitary bridge lay in tack surrounded by fire on both sides. Rota looked to his right observing the continuous fire being poured down to the waiting troops on the far distance bank of the river. Rota counted the amount of enemy activity which was lying round after round across the bridge. The situation for the troop, who had travailed hundreds of miles and had seen death and destruction at is best could not have been in a worst predicament that they were in now.

The small corps which the troop had managed to get to was well concealed from the concert bombardment, due to it dead ground and forward slops it made the perfect location in attempting the 4 kms drive to the bridge. Even as Sgt Normal examined the changed landscape there was a flurry of explosions around the village which lay cross the bridge. It was like watching the silent movie of another war. The barrage intensified as though some artillery observer had called for it. Lt Small now saw the artillery were, now ranging on individual targets. He saw one challenger swerve to avoid a deep crater, only to collide with another which had moved to close. He could almost feel the grinding of the metal against metal, but the vehicles separated with a barely noticeable lowering of their speed.

Lt Small looked at Sgt Normal in a knowing jester that spelled out the burning question on how we are going to get across the bridge. Deep down he new that the only option for the troop was for one challenger to act as a rear guard action while the other two ran the gauntlet to safety. Rota looked the way the troop would take; there was a long straight road with a few isolated houses on one side and a low, red—brick buildings on the other. As far as the eye could see the country was as flat as a billiard table, and Rota thought with dismay of trying to fight a tank battle in this sort of country, where the enemy could see you coming from several miles away. Sgt Normal told Dave Tuesday to see if hey could contact the battle group, Dave popped his head in the turret and started, a few moment later Dave appeared with a look that said it all, still no contact.

Monty Kean tapped Rota leg, "What up Monty" "I need a pee" Rota climbed out from his commanders seat and stood on the NBC pack watching Monty slowly rise his arms to pull him self out though the hatch. He looked tried with deep red eyes caused by concert glare though the sights. Next to climbed out was Ulta her shirt buttons open to revolve he cleavage, Rota noticed that the slight cool of the morning air made her nipples erect. Ulta stood on the loaders step and fasted her buttons up before descending down the turret.

Sgt Rota Normal climbed down from the rear of the challenger and walked to the edge Of the wood with map in hand. Cpl Jones followed him. Staple new that his troop

Sergeant had worked a plain on how the troop would cross; it was just a matter of time, before he told us all.

3 Troop gathered at the rear of Sgt Normal challenger. Lt Small handed out the fags so Sgt Normal could out line the plain of action. Rota told the troop that the situation which they had all come though hand ended with a situation that was against them unless we took out the rear echelon which was bombarding the bridge along with our battle group, the only way which this could be archived was for one of us to act as rear guard while the others made a dash for the river. Harry Young along with Monty Kean looked at each other then said quietly "it be us" Lt Small broke the silence to inform the troop that the challenger which would act as rear guard would be Sgt Normal. Rota blow out a long smoke trail before he said" both challengers would cross over all ammo expect for three HESH for each" This would give Rota and his crew seven APFSDS and ten HESH. Once Lt Small and Cpl Jones came out of the dead ground they would fire board side together at the enemy's location, this we hope shall draw fire to you but at the same time

Sgt Normal will engaged them from the rear, any question? The troops for the first time were silent, each with their own thought of what had just been said. Rota's crew climbed aboard ready to reserve the ammo. Ulta stayed out the way of the rear load, in a way Ulta had her own thought of what would happen to her if they became captured. She new she would be tortured before they shot her. Her family would all so be arrested and then be put to death. Ulta looked at the movement of the troop carrying the projectiles from one challenger to the other as if they had become a column of ants. The last round was stowed away ready to be launched against the next target. All three commanders had there final brief before turning towards their challengers.

 Sgt Rota Normal was the last to leave the for ward edge of the wood, he turned his head to look at the other two commanders, would he ever see them again. Rota mind racing back to the start of this conflict the happy times they had spent in the cellar bar after a days shooting. The troop had bonded well during these past days of carnage the last engagement was upon them. Rota walked back to his challenger his crew waiting. Harry Young smoking his last fag looked at his commander and smiled before he produced a beer from be hide his back. Each of his crew did the same beer in hand. Ulta had Rota's open and ready "cheers" The challenger crew downed the beer in one mouth full before taken air back in to their lungs, as one they tossed the now empty bottles to the waiting trees smashing in unison, a thunderous sound echoed amongst the slight prying eyes of the trees. With smiles all around the challenger crew of Sgt Rota Normal climbed aboard. With both engines on line gun kit on they slow reversed pasted Lt Small and Cpl Jones both commanders stared at the passing challenger watching it until it disappeared into dead ground

Chapter Nineteen

Last Round Fired

Day Firthteen 09th September

Once they had left the confines of the wood far be hide them Sgt Normal headed west using dead as he went. Rota had worked out that by doing this he would be able to approach the enemy and not been seen. Rota had crawled the challenger to the steep slope above the fallen tree, to the point where he could witness his next engagement. He could hear the sound of the engines in the idle mould, a generator in the distance through the trees. The sky was brighter, the sun rising beyond the tall horizon of the woodland. Sitting with his head set removed Rota froze, a few feet to his right leaves rustled, he relaxed as a terrified rodent scurried away through the undergrowth. There were other hunters ready to strike its deadly blow upon the waiting pray.

Sgt Normal eased the challenger forward leaving the rodent to find it's on pray. He could soon start to smell diesel fuel, exhaust fumes along with cordite from the exploding artillery bombardment and the throbbing sound of the engines which grew louder. There were men beyond the clumps of bracken and bramble that skirted the clearing around the waiting enemy. Rota could see the head and shoulders of a guard patrolling the edge of the wood. He knew there must be others concealed throughout the forest.

Sgt Rota Normal and his crew took a long time to inch the challenger forward until at least he had a clear view of the encampment. What he saw was vehicles parked close to the trees on the side farthest away from him. Rota recognized the radio vehicle with its dish aerials, a few meters from it was a BTR command post on the left and isolated, this would be his first target, get them knocked out and the situation would be cerotic.

Rota traversed the main barrel left then right showing Monty Kean the targets which needed to be engaged first. Dave Tuesday loaded HESH, loaders guard made ready. Ulta, loaded the GPMG, she was ready. Sgt Normal looked at his watch he noticed that the hands said it was 07.30am. Rota pressed his CPU and sent a message to Lt Small informing him he was about to engage as soon as the first round had found its target they were to pull out and head for the bridge, the net went silent.

FIRE lasing FIRING NOW before the first round hit the BTR Rota witnessed a commander exit the rear of the vehicle the explosion lifted him clean of his feet, the vacuum of the explosion tour his body in half sending parts in all directions. The round had done its job sending vehicle debris into the radio vehicle, one round two hit. Monty traversed of to the waiting Pion 257 Artillery, he had missed the destruction of the BTR but heard Rota's shout of satisfaction. Again the round found its target sending vehicle parts flying though the air only to land amongst the already burning carnage which was now littering the wood. The challenger lurched forward after firing the APFSDS, this time Monty had fired more calmly. The round struck the T80 just under the thick Sloping armour of its bow, and exploded on impact. The vehicle stopped as though it had run into an impenetrable wall, a second later Monty saw one of it crew bale out apparently unwounded, leaping from the turret only to be brought down by a hale of 7.62mm, the challenger turret was moving again as Monty sought another target.

Lt Small hearing the sound of the engagement eased both challenger's out though the wood. His direction was the reverse slop directly to his front. Both challengers once they had hit the road traversed of board side. Out though the dead ground came a sight really seen in modern war fair, here were two main battle tanks the challenger, both main armament traversed of in unison as if they were connected together. On the signal from Lt Small both engaged sending HESH rounds to the waiting targets which Sgt Normal was engaging in. Both challengers rocked from side to side sending out a puff of smoke from each barrel, this continued until they had expanded all their ammo, what followed next was the engagement of the GPMG sending round after round at the uninspected foe causing carnage at the feeling infantrymen trying to find what cover they could, they where brought down their crimson blood spreading though the grass like wide follower. The on lookers across the bridge could not be leave what they had witnessed, before they new what was happening both challengers had crossed the bridge to safety.

'Shit!' Monty swore, not at Normal but because the burst of the challenger's 120mm round was ahead and to the right of the T80. As Monty brought the sight onto it again, he suddenly realized with horror that he was staring right down the black muzzle barrel of the T 80's gun. There was a burst of flame from the barrel of its 125mm, and Monty instinctively ducked instead of firing.

'Monty! What the blood hell?' shouted Rota? There was an explosion on the slope forty meters to the rear of the challenger. Harry Young didn't see it, but he felt the ground shake and the violent thud of the pressure wave against the hull of the challenger. The shell must have passed the turret within centimetres before it landed. Monty quickly brought his sights back on to the target again the challenger's gun roared. This time the round found its mark sending part of its turret flying leaving be hind a clear view of what used to be a fighting machine. Monty could see what was left of the commander; the bottom part of his body was where he had been sat the rest of his torso had gone with the turret. "Stop Loading, load HEAH shouted Rota" Loaded" reported Dave. On Lasing, Firing Now, Monty pressed the barker firing switch and heard the satisfying response from the gun; the round tore the group of infantry apart sending dirt and fragment of bone in all direction, what was left in side the crater lay motionless. Monty had the main sight on another T80, which had appeared though the smoke, before he had said the word "ON" the shell had found its mark on the challenger's turret. The shell had been directed upwards which saved them but the damage had been done. The cupola hatch along with most of the episcope had been blown apart sending fragment of metal back wards to the rear, parts of the hatch landed on the gear box decks. Monty tried to traverse to engage the T80 before a second shell finished them. Again and again Monty tried; the turret had got caught up with parts of the hatch. Sgt Rota Normal lay slumped forward on his sight, the shell and the explosion had knocked his head forward temporally causing him to black out. Dave Tuesday reached over to check him, blood was trickling down his for head blinding him in both eyes, Ulta handed Dave a bandage to ease the flow of blood. Dave looked at Monty then started to climbed Out though the loaders hatch, he knew the only chance they had, was to remove the objet which was preventing the turret from traversing. While Dave was outside the turret Rota came round and looked at the sate of his cupola, he turned his head and looked at Ulta she had blood on her hands and jacket, had she been hit thought Rota, then he felt his head and realised that the blood was his. Rota s mind was wondering why there were only three of them inside the turret. Monty was shouting though the intercom to get Harry to revise; with all this going on Sgt Rota Normal was oblivion in what was happing out side the challenger. Harry Young revised the challenger down the slop into dead ground. Dave Tuesday legs dangled though the hatch before Rota saw his smiling face, "what been going on Dave"

    Dave Tuesday explained the best he could before Harry Young warred Rota that a T80 barrel had just popped up to their right flank. Sgt Normal twisted his score head to the right at the same time grabbing his duplex control to line the barrel up with the target. Loaded shouted Dave, what with? HEAH last one reported Dave. Monty lased the T80 and waited until he was belly up before he pressed his firing button. The round sailed true towards the target, the impact lifted the tank clean of its tracks before it came down with a bump. Rota saw the commanders hatch fly open with smoke bellowing out though it. The commander stopped and looked towards the challenger before he tried to climbed down the side of his tank, he was cut down by Monty's fire of the GMPG his motionless body hung in mid fight before it fell earth wards to the all ready burning grass. Sgt Normal traversed forward and told Harry to pull hard right stick then to follow the ridge line. Once Rota was satisfied he had moved a good distance from his last position he told Harry to pull up to the ridge line.

    With a turret up position Sgt Normal could see what carnage he and his crew had done. The tree line was scattered with burning vehicles along with deformed body's which were once human. Rota made out that one IV13 and a Pion257 Artillery piece was still engaging the bridge. "What's the state of the ammo Dave?" Dave quickly counted up "3APFSDS, 2 BOXES OF 7.62" Okay Monty take out the Pion then the BRDM make them count. Monty had the main sight on the Pion "Take your time." "Sod . . . . The bastards gone" "No he hasn't your laid on the wrong target—traverse right ON". "Okay sarge seen" The challenger heaved upwards with the shock as the gunner hit the firing button and the propulsion charge detonated in the breech. With the challenger engine on tick-over the roar of the gun was impressive within the confines of the fighting compartment; smoke from the muzzle blurred their vision for a few seconds. Once it cleared the Pion 257 with it barrel bent in half laid with the rest of the fallen. Monty caught sight of the remaining IV13 Command vehicle trying to make a run for it, part of the way the IV13 was in dead ground until it emerged 2000meters away, Monty remembering to arm off on a moving target fired his last but one round. The Command Vehicle tilted to the right before it settled back on its wheels, the rear door flung open, Monty waited for the crew to emerge only to witness a ball of flame escaping from the dark depths with in. The fight had ended. Sgt Normal looked at the burning hulk not noticing a lone T80 emerged though the smoke, he fired his shell which found it make. The shells torn away the TOGS system, which is to the right and forward of the commander taken with it was the stowage basket part of the turret armour leaving a jagged hole which exposed Rota to the elements, along with this the commanders hatch what was left of it went flying along with this the remaining parts of the cupola.

Monty had seen it just before the T80 had fired his deadly shell; the last APFSDS hit the T80 square on above the drivers hatch. The turret lifted from it roller bearings sending it side wards before coming to rest. A few moments later an explosion could be heard with in the turret sending shells and small arms rounds flying skywards. The silence befell the turret after the last round was fired, the only sound to be heard was the breech making its final cluck sound resting in the open position ready to receive its next projectile. Smell of cordite filled the turret though the now open breech, sending in cool fresh air. Ulta looked across the vast space of the turret towards Rota; he lay motionless looking though his commander's sight.

The sky had brightened and the cloud was now broken so that patches of sunlight drifted across the open ground, chasing the columns of dark smoke spiralling from the battle debris. He could see only one living being amongst it all; four hundred meters away a solitary infantryman, still wearing his helmet no weapon wandered aimlessly in the open. Rota looked closely and realised that this figure of a human being had only one arm, his crimson blood falling on *to* the scorched earth he wouldn't last long his last dream of home was fading fast.

Dave Tuesday gently eased Sgt Normal away from his sights; his right shoulder had a penetrating wound, blood was dripping down his arm making a sound like a tap hadn't been switched of when it hit the floor plate. Ulta came behind the breech she could feel the cool air swirling though the rifling of the barrel, she reached upwards to touch Rota. Sgt Rota Normal turned, his face covered in pain managed to smile, before the cracking sound of the net echoed though the head sets. Lt Small was calling. Dave Tuesday answered "send over." After, the call Dave removed his head set and looked at the sate of the turret, then at Monty who still had his eyes fixed to his sights before he told the crew what the Troop Leader had said.

Sgt Normal was told that his approach to the bridge would be covered, and it was time for him and his crew to come home. Rota just sat back in his commander's seat, taking in what had been said, by the troop leader. He looked around the turret and the three members of the turret crew, apart from the damage to his cupola the inside looked normal. Rota slowly placed his head set on, pressed his CPU and told his troop leader they were coming home.

Chapter Twenty

Guard Room

The alarm clock went of at 05.30am; Sgt Rota Normal turned over opened one eye and starred long at the flashing numbers before he realised it meant some thing, he turned on his back eyes closed nursing the worst hang over he had had for a very long time. Rota eased his feet out of the bed slowly placing them on to the bed side carpet. Once he had stood up, he let the blood flow down to wards his feet, before he walked over towards the window. Rota pulled the curtains opened, it was raining. Great he thought what a day to do a guard duty. Turning away from the rain which was lashing against his window he wondered over to where his towel hung on the door. Rota wrapped it around his naked body and made his way down the long corridor towards the showers. The warm feel of the shower running down felt good, Rota placed his hands on the shower wall and watched the water disappear down the drain. After a while he reached up and turned the shower handle of, turned around and placed his head in to his towel, eyes closed thinking of the night which he had just had. Wrapping now the damp towel around him he walked towards the sink, Rota stopped and looked hard at his body noticing the scar on his forehead and right shoulder. Sgt Normal lifted his arm to feel the tender purple marks, drifting into a day dream remembering how he had got the scars, the sound of the water cascading on to the wash room floor brought Rota back to the land of the living. He clasped both hands together and slashed water on to his face to start the shaving process. Satisfied that he looked the part Rota made the long walk back to his room.

Sgt Rota Normal looked around the room for his beret, it dawned on him that he had lost it a few days ago. Finding his spare one Rota made saw that it covered his scar on his forehead before he opened his bunk door and then made his way down stairs. Before Rota opened the door to the out side world, he turned and looked at him self in the mirror. Once out side standing on the porch Sgt

Normal looked in both directions before turning left towards the guard room.

It was still raining hard when he stepped on to the foot path; Rota gazed up wards to the dark clouds and the falling rain, tinny droplet landed on his open eyes. He quickly closed them quizzing them shut wiping away the rain. The long walk to the guard room seemed to take for ever, the only sound breaking the silence was the sound of his own boots echoing along the foot path, until he heard the formulary sound of the guard falling in outside the guard room.

Sgt Normal turned the corner; the guard was stood to attention waiting for him, at the front of the parade was Cpl Staple Jones. Rota smiled knowing the next 24 hours would be spent in the company of his troop. Staple handed the guard over to Rota, he quickly walked down the line, inspecting as he went. At the end of the line stood Troopers Kean and Young, both smiled as he walked passed them. Rota marched to the front of the guard, halted and waited for the approach of the orderly officer. Staple gave the nod that the orderly officer was coming. Rota brought the guard back up to attention, turned to his left and waited. The orderly officer he noticed was his troop leader. Rota set of towards him, both came to a halt at the same time, saluted exchanged words, saluted again then marched towards the guard. The troop leader like Rota inspected the guard force, satisfied that the guard were in good order they both marched to the front and halted. Sgt Rota Normal gave the command for the guard to fall out. Once in side the guard room Rota checked the DOB, he noticed that an entry had been made concerning a woman asking for him, it gave no details of what the woman wonted apart that she would call again, he looked to see what her name was, and none was given. Puzzled by the entry he turned the pages and closed the book.

Monty Kean came from the back of the guard room carrying a black coffee, he handed it over to Sgt Normal who looked like he could do with one, thought Monty.

Staple Jones organised the stag rota for the day putting Kean and Young on together, making saw that they did the last stag.

Sgt Rota Normal was feeling the strain of the night before, his eye's felling heavy his head was aching it was time he got his head down. On reaching one of the cells Rota slowly closed the door behind him covered his head with the blanket and drifted of to sleep.

While Sgt Normal was away it was time for Harry Young and Monty Kean to do the gate. They had only been out for a short while when they noticed this woman approaching. Harry noticed that she had a slight limp to her left leg and she was wearing one of the regiment berets, apart from that they both thought she was very attractive. The woman stopped short of them, then asked if they could tell her if Sgt Rota Normal was on guard to day, Harry said he was. The woman smiling thanked them. Before she entered the gate the woman stopped and slowly turned her head and looked again at Harry and then at Monty, with a smile on her face she opened the gate and walked to the window, she was home.

Cpl Staple Jones reading the paper looked up when she came to the window. He smiled, he thought he had seen her some where before, but couldn't remember were, not saying a word until she asked to see Sgt Rota Normal. Staple eased himself out of his chair and made his way to the rear of the guard room. The cell which Rota was in, was the last one on the right, the door was still closed. Staple opening it slowly rocked Rota awake. "What wrong Staple" asked Rota? Staple explained that a woman was waiting at the desk for him, the same one who was in the DOB, Rota said that he would be there in a few minutes.

Staple Jones turned around and stated to walk back to the front desk. Before Staple had time to close the door to the cell, Rota, rubbing the sleep from his eyes called out and asked what her name was? Staple just smiled and uttered the name ULTA.

The End

Was this story real or just a dream—the choice it yours

GLOSSARY

BAOR	British Army of the Rhine
OP	Operator
C/S	Call Sign
BFBS	British Forces Broadcasting Service
SQN	Squadron
SSM	Squadron Sargent Major
LAD	Light Ade Detachment
SSGT	Staff Sargent
432	Tracked vehicle used by the LAD
SqnLdr	Squadron Leader (Major)
SHQ	Squadron Headquarters
2i/c	Second in Command
SQMS	Squadron Quartermaster Sargent
MBT	Main Battle Tank
APFSDS	Armour Piercing Fin Stabilised Discarding Sabot
HESH	High Explosive Squash Head
GUE	Generator Unit Engine
LT	Lieutenant
REME	Royal Electrical Mechanical Engineers
GPMG	General Purpose Machine Gun 7.62mm
TOGS	Thermal Observation Gunnery System
FSG	Fire Support Group
SGT	Sargent
NBC	Nuclear Biological Chemical
CPU	Commanders Presell Unit
Net	Radio
BV	Boiling Vessel
DOB	Daily Occurrence Book (Guard Room)

Gary Kent joined the Royal Horse Guards/1st Dragoons in 1973. Serving on the Chieftain and Challenger Main Battle tank, in 2011 he published his first book his, Auto Biography titled "24 Year Colour Service" He now lives with his family in Lincolnshire after retiring from the Armed Forces in 2012.

Printed in Great Britain
by Amazon.co.uk, Ltd.,
Marston Gate.